"What happens if you hate living with me?"

"I won't. You could hate living with me, though."

She shook her head. "No, I won't. I've been thinking the dumbest things, Mitch. Our toothbrushes together . . ."

"Our shoes side by side . . . Nina, it will be so fine and great living together. Don't you think so?" he said anxiously.

She put her hands on his shoulders so that they were looking at each other full face. "Okay," she said after a moment.

"Okay?" A smile broke over his face.

She nodded. How extraordinary, how wonderful, to be able to make someone else so happy!

The Laundromat was packed by now. Standing by the steamy window, they put their arms around each other in a long, warm hug. *I'm going to remember this*, Nina thought. *I'll never forget this moment.*

NORMA FOX MAZER is the author of many well-known books for young adults, including *Up in Seth's Room*; *Dear Bill, Remember Me?*; *Summer Girls, Love Boys*; *Saturday, the Twelfth of October*; and *A Figure of Speech*, all available in Laurel-Leaf editions, and *I, Trissy*, available in a Yearling edition. She lives in Jamesville, New York.

Someone to Love

Norma Fox Mazer

LAUREL-LEAF BOOKS bring together under a single imprint outstanding works of fiction and nonfiction particularly suitable for young adult readers, both in and out of the classroom. Charles F. Reasoner, Professor Emeritus of Children's Literature and Reading, New York University, is consultant to this series.

Published by
Dell Publishing
a division of
Bantam Doubleday Dell Publishing Group, Inc.
666 Fifth Avenue
New York, New York 10103

ISBN: 0-440-98062-3

RL: 5.0

Reprinted by arrangement with Delacorte Press

Printed in the United States of America

One Previous Edition

June 1989

10 9 8 7 6 5 4 3 2 1

KRI

For Norma Klein

". . . of making many books there is no end."

Chapter One

The first time Nina Bloom really noticed Mitch was about the fourth day he'd been painting the house next door. All the houses on University Avenue were huge wooden things; three, four, or even five stories high, with big, rambling front porches that always looked ready to collapse. They had once been elegant one-family homes. Now they were cut up into dozens of little apartments filled with students from Rhodes University.

The house Nina lived in—next to the one being painted—had a name, The Lion's Arms; but except for the name there was nothing to distinguish it from any other house on the block. The second-floor apartment Nina shared with two other students was small and dark. Nina's room wasn't much more than a windowless closet. The dim stairs and hallway outside the apartment were filled with ancient smells of moldy wood and cooked meat. Walk into any apartment building on University Avenue and you smelled the same odors, saw the same graffiti, and heard the same music.

The building next to The Lion's Arms was being painted a lurid raspberry. That was the first thing Nina noticed that day as she headed down the street on her way back from campus. Next she focused on the painter who was standing on a scaffold, paint can by his side. And after that, how could she not help but notice the almost gleeful way he was slapping on the paint?

Up came the loaded paintbrush. *Splaat!* Paint hit the clapboards. Then quickly the splotch of paint was smoothed out, the painter's wrist snapping back and forth as he swooped the brush across the worn boards. *Splaat!* Another brushload. Nina slowed down her usually precipitous, head-thrust-forward walk to enjoy the show.

No sooner had she done so than the painter turned around and, out of all the people on the street, looked at her. A big smile spread across his face, and he lifted one hand in a jaunty salute. "Hi!" Flustered, Nina nodded jerkily and ran into her building, knapsack bouncing on her back.

Going up the stairs, she rolled her eyes at her own naiveté. Would she ever learn to be casual? Easy with herself, and men, and the world?

"Oh, hi," Sonia said as Nina came in, and she went on talking on the phone, giving out little tinkling laughs that meant a guy was on the other end of the line. Emmett rubbed against Nina's ankle. "Hi, my big cat-baby." In the kitchen she fed him, not forgetting to put his bowl in a corner where it wouldn't be under Lynell's nose.

"Was that D.G.?" she said when Sonia came into the kitchen. She took hamburger from the refrigerator and made a patty. "No," Sonia said. "It wasn't."

Sitting on the table, Sonia swung her legs and ate from a cup of yogurt. Her nails were painted green. She had a round, sensuous face, which she made up meticulously every morning. "Wait, wait," she'd call to Lynell, who, always ready first, would be standing impatiently by the door. "Wait, I'm still putting on my face."

Her first day on campus Nina had gone by mistake into the music building, and there she had seen a posted notice for a roommate. MUSTN'T MIND SMALL ROOM. NO SMOKERS!

Tall Lynell, short Sonia. Like Mutt and Jeff, they had stood in the doorway of their apartment and alternated asking Nina questions. Was she neat? She definitely didn't smoke? Did she do drugs? "Is your cat well behaved?" That from Lynell, fine-boned, stern, a bit remote.

"He's a good cat."

"Do you realize what it means to live with two music students?" Sonia was earnest, smiling directly into Nina's eyes. "I sing, and Lynell plays the flute. We do that here, in this apartment."

"I like music. I admit, I don't know much about it, but—"

"You know what you like," Lynell finished.

"Well . . . yes," Nina said. Was that funny? Lynell and Sonia laughed.

"The apartment is tiny tiny."

"I don't care."

"No place to spread out."

"I've always shared a room with my sister."

"Where did you say you come from?"

"Hawley. In the Adirondacks? Real small town?" At their blank looks, she added, unnecessarily, "A creek runs through it."

"Do people really still say *crick*?" Sonia asked. She looked at Lynell.

Lynell shrugged, smiled. Then, "Let's have a glass of wine. Do you like wine?"

"Yes," Nina said.

"Good," Lynell said, and Nina knew she had passed whatever the test was.

To a certain extent Nina believed in fate—the same way, really, that she believed in God: she didn't dare not believe. Wasn't it fate that Sonia had posted that roommate-wanted notice only hours before Nina wandered into the music building? Wasn't it fate that Nina had been the first person to show up at their door? And wasn't it fate that, although Lynell was unenthusiastic about Emmett, Sonia was an animal lover and considered Emmett a plus? And finally, wasn't it fate that the university was so overcrowded that the Director of Housing quickly agreed to refund Nina's deposit so someone else could have her assigned dormitory room?

Those first days Nina was enamored of her new

roommates. Beautiful, fabulous creatures! Sonia, dimpled and bosomy; Lynell, slender, standing often on one foot, a waterfall of golden brown hair down her back. How perfectly suited Lynell seemed to the slender silver flute. And when Sonia, hands pressed to her chest, opened her mouth, a honey sound poured out, stunning Nina. She longed for them all to become best friends.

It hadn't worked out that way. Six weeks had passed, and Nina was lonely. She reproached herself. Why wasn't she more forthcoming?

Just the other night, for instance, the other two girls had decided at the last moment to try for tickets to a chamber music concert. As they bustled around getting ready, Nina sat at the window with Emmett in her lap. Because they didn't specifically say, "Nina, you'll come, won't you?" did it mean they didn't want her?

Emmett touched her face with his paw. He sensed her feelings and often comforted her.

"I'm ready," Lynell said, coming out of the bedroom. She was wearing an embroidered shawl and a long skirt.

Sonia looked at her. "I feel drab."

"Poor little drab bird," Lynell mocked, linking her arm with Sonia's. "See you later, Nina." They went out.

Nina wondered if, when the two of them had met at age twelve in a summer music camp, they had even then presented such a striking physical contrast. And if, right away, they had struck up their friendship and evolved their own special kind of communication.

Lynell only had to say "Sonia, did you—?" for Sonia to answer "I told you I would."

Of course, Nina told herself, she couldn't expect not to be a *bit* of an outsider. But in truth, it wasn't only with her roommates that she felt this way. She had become acutely aware of how little she knew about a whole range of subjects—and how restricted her life had been. She stayed up late studying and woke up early worrying about marks and papers and all the books on her reading lists. She was keeping up, but was never at ease, terrified all the time of failing. To fail would be worse than the failure itself: it would mean going back home with her head hanging, back to Community College of the Mountains, where she'd spent her first year, back to her parents' house, where her father still wore his invalid's slippers and her mother, bitter and proud, kept what remained of their family together.

Lynell was a Californian: she looked it, looked like the lean, smooth girls Nina had seen in magazines and on TV. Lynell had lived with her family all over the United States, and Sonia, too, had traveled, had visited Mexico, England, and France. *Do people really still say 'crick'?* Yes, they did. But not Nina, not anymore. Not unless she forgot, anyway. And she was working, too, on her country-mouse accent. She noticed that Lynell said toe-mah-toe and awnt. She, born and bred in the same small town in Upstate New York, said toe-*maay*-toe and aaahnt.

She got along well enough with Lynell and Sonia, but she still felt alone. They had each other, and boyfriends as well. Sonia's husky D.G. and Lynell's aristocratic Adam. Nina? She was nineteen and had no one. Had never had someone special and close. There was a hunger in her, a hunger for a friend and a lover. For a loving friend.

In the hall now the door slammed. *"Emmett."* It was Lynell. "Nina," she called from the hall, "get this cat."

Nina scooped up Emmett. Old and half blind, the dear fellow was always trying to get out of the apartment and down to the street. Whenever he heard someone at the door, he was there, waiting, hoping to escape. He weighed twenty-five pounds, had a tail striped like a raccoon's, and had been Nina's for more than ten years. Maybe she shouldn't have brought him to college, but at home her sister, Nancy, didn't care about him, and her mother had no time.

Lynell set down her flute case. "The catbox is starting to smell," she remarked.

"I'm changing the litter today."

"Good."

"Guess who called *me*," Sonia said. Lynell took off her beret, and she and Sonia went into the room they shared.

Nina wandered into the living room, eating her hamburger rolled up in a piece of soft white bread. Music came up from the record store across the way. Horns blared; cyclists and joggers wove in and out of the crowds. Three boys in jeans and gum boots almost danced down the street. A girl balanced her books on her head. Nina leaned out the window, watching. In the air was the smell of hot dogs and exhaust fumes. Her first days on campus she had wandered in a daze through the mobs of students, thinking, *Where do I belong? What am I doing here? Am I going to make it?* Yet by now it was as if she'd always been here, living in this apartment on this street and moving from class to class in the huge, limestone, Gothic buildings.

Emmett stood up on his back legs and put his paws on her lap. She fed him a piece of hamburger. He liked ketchup, too. She picked him up and kissed him, but after a moment he squirmed to be free.

In the bedroom she heard Sonia and Lynell laughing together and thought of going in and saying, "Guess what happened to *me* today? The painter talked to me." But remembering her awkwardness, she thought that even if she tried to make a funny story of it to amuse them, it wouldn't come out right.

Every day that week Nina saw the painter up on the scaffolding, slapping paint on the old boards. And every day that week he saw her. He was watching her. She hurried past him in the morning and again in the evening, her head ducked, blushing and blowing hair out of her eyes. Sometimes, though, she sneaked a glance at him. Couldn't tell much with him covered in white overalls and that cap pulled down over his head, except that he was tall and young.

On Friday he spoke to her. "Your coat's on inside out," he said. She didn't realize he was speaking to her. "Up here," he called. "Look up here." Then he came down the ladder. "Hi. Did you hear me? Your name's on inside out."

"What?" She blew hair out of her eyes, laughed. "My name?"

He put down his can of paint. "I mean your rain-coat—you're wearing it inside out."

She looked down at the yellow slicker with Richie's name stenciled across the front and saw that he was right. "Well," she said, embarrassed, and glanced furtively at her sneakers, hoping her laces weren't untied.

"Hi," he said. "I'm Mitch." There was a big splash of raspberry paint down the front of his overalls. Above the bill of his white cap RUSTOLA CLEANS RUST was printed in red letters. "You could use a haircut, too," he said.

Although he was smiling, this bothered her, and she walked quickly by and up the stairs of her building. "Wait, you didn't tell me your name," he called after her.

Later that evening she found a pair of scissors and recklessly chopped at her bangs, which, it was true, were always falling into her eyes. When she put down the scissors, she saw, with a creaking heart, that she looked as ragged and frayed as an old blanket.

Chapter Two

"I almost didn't go to classes today," Nina said. She and Kim Ogun, who was in her lit class, were sitting on the grass near the granite goddess with her arms outflung. It was hot for October; above them the sky was a pure, hard blue.

"I know what you mean. I couldn't face the library today." Kim was freckled and round-faced.

Nina lay back in the grass, hands behind her head. "Do you dream a lot, Kim?"

"I don't think I ever dream."

"You don't! I'm always dreaming!" Last night she had dreamed she was home, in the backyard. There was the sandbox from her childhood; she knelt down and ran sand through her fingers. Then she noticed she had no clothes on and became worried that her mother would scold her. At that moment the painter appeared, but the odd thing was that his cheeks were rough from acne. And this made Nina feel sorry for him and at the same time really tender. She stroked his arm and said, "There, now, it'll be okay."

"It is *inhuman* to study today," Kim said. "I refuse. I go on strike. I will *not* study."

"I have to write a paper for Professor Lehman," Nina said languidly. She had found it nearly impossible to concentrate today. The dream lingered, and the sky, so blue and big, filled her with longing.

"El Professoro Lehman iss a darling," Kim said. "Nina! Don't you think he's darling? Love his class. I hope I get an A on my paper. I'd like to impress the *hell* out of him."

They turned to watch two boys jogging past in brief running shorts. "Darling," Kim said.

Staring up at the sky, Nina thought that Professor Lehman's eyes were that same blue. He was her favorite teacher. Her first day in his class she'd thought he looked exactly the way a professor should look— worn tweed jacket, salt and pepper beard, and he even had a pipe. His manner, too, was satisfying. As he lectured he roamed the room, streaking his hands through his hair, pulling at his tie, and pounding desks to make his point.

Sometimes when his eyes roamed restlessly toward the back of the room where she sat Nina imagined that he was speaking to her. Then she sat up straight to give him her most devoted attention. But it was precisely at those moments that she heard and re-membered the least.

After she and Kim parted, Nina walked home more slowly than usual, reluctant to leave the sky behind and go into the dim apartment. Passing the sandwich shop on the corner, she looked in and saw the painter standing at the counter. At once her dream returned to her. Her neck became warm, and almost without thinking, she walked in, walked toward him. *I'm sleepwalking*, she thought, trying to understand what she was doing. The moment the bell on the door chimed, she wanted to run out. But the painter had seen her.

"Yes?" the woman at the counter said.

"Dr Pepper, please," Nina said.

"Hi," the painter said. "Remember me?"

Nina turned as if seeing him for the first time. "Oh!" she said brightly. "Hello."

"I'm painting the house on your block," he said.

"I know." He didn't have acne at all. He was taller than she remembered and had a good smile, showing very white teeth.

"I'm Mitch," he said.

Nina nodded, smiling down into her Dr Pepper, hit by a sudden wave of shyness.

"I don't know your name, though," he said.

"Nina," she said.

"Nina what?"

"Bloom."

"Bloom? Nina Bloom?"

"Yes, Bloom," she said, and for some reason she

repeated it, this time in a loud, confident voice. "Bloom."

"Nina Bloom Bloom, can I buy you another Dr Pepper?"

"I still haven't finished this one."

"Well, another for when you do finish?" And he ordered a Dr Pepper for her and an orange soda for himself. They took the drinks to a little table by the window and sat down. "What luck that you came in," he said.

"Not exactly luck," she blurted. "I saw you in here."

"You followed me in?" He smiled delightedly.

"I don't usually follow guys around," she said in that same confident voice that was hers, yet took her by surprise.

"Even better," he said. "Nina Bloom Bloom, what are you toting in that huge knapsack?"

"Books, mostly. Junk for classes . . ."

"I thought so. You're a student, right? You go to Rhodes. I did, too, last year."

"What was your major?" She assumed he'd graduated, and was not surprised that the only job he could find was house painting. Jobs were scarce.

"Pre-law. I dropped out in my junior year."

"Why?"

"Complicated. Has to do with a lot of things—me, my family. I'll tell you the whole story sometime. I'd rather hear about you right now, Nina." He pronounced it, Neenah. Soft. At home they said Nee-nuh.

"I cut my hair," Nina said, again blurting things in a way that made her blush. But she couldn't stop.

"Your hair? You cut your hair?"

"After you said— Well, it seemed so shaggy. Always in my eyes." She brushed at her bangs.

"No, you shouldn't have," he said. "On my say-so? No, you shouldn't have," he repeated.

"Well . . . it needed it anyway."

He took off his white cap, put it on the table. He had masses of curly hair, gleaming, brown, healthy-looking curls. "Neenah," he said. "What year are you in, Nina?"

"I'm a sophomore."

"Do you like it?" He sat back, hands clasped behind his neck. He was a bit thin, even stringy, and she wondered if he ate enough.

"I do. I like it a lot," she said. "But it's much harder than Community College." Then she had to tell him all about her first year at the Community College of the Mountains, and her hometown, and somehow she even told him how she'd decided to go to college only because her tenth grade guidance counselor was so sure she couldn't make it.

"Mr. Pretorious—we called him Mr. Pretty behind his back—filled out my schedule, and without even asking me he gave me Typing, Shorthand, and Business Arithmetic." Nina had had no other thought herself, but she'd been outraged that he had done that without consulting her. "I said, 'Why did you give me those subjects?' And he said, 'You'll be going to work after you graduate, won't you? I *hope* you're planning to graduate, Nina.' That was a dig at my brother, who dropped out before graduation to join the Navy.

"I was mad. I said, 'I'm going to college. I'm going

to Rhodes! Put me in the college entrance classes!' It was the first *I'd* heard about my college plans, but I sat there as if I'd thought it all out. 'Well,' Mr. P. said, 'maybe Community College for a year or so.' I can remember just how he opened a drawer, looked inside, and then closed it, his head shaking back and forth all the time. It was as if no matter what I said, he was telling me, *No way, girl, you'll never make it!* You know, Mitch, in our school the teachers called the kids Buzzards and Bluebirds. You can guess who they thought was college material."

Mitch leaned toward Nina. "Did you ever notice how many people deal in stereotypes? Clichéd thinking? My father's a professor, so everyone has always assumed I'd go to college. Become a professor, too. I always loved working with my hands. There are other things in life besides college. Only nobody ever bothered to tell me that."

"And nobody bothered to tell me that there *was* college. I guess because we were from the Buzzard side of town. You know, I have this impulsive streak, but I really surprised myself that morning. There I was, sitting in Mr. P.'s office, and I hear myself saying in this loud voice, 'I'm going to college!' "

And all at once Nina heard herself *now,* her enthusiasm, the words tumbling out, the way her voice rose indignantly as she said Mr. Pretty's name. Her face flushed, she pushed the Dr Pepper can around in a wet spot. "I've been gabbing; I don't usually."

"I liked it," Mitch said. "I enjoyed it, I want to hear more. Listen, did that bum ever apologize to you, or say anything?"

"Mr. Pretty?" Nina laughed. "He wouldn't. Maybe I should send him a card. 'Hope you are well, and just to let you know I DID IT!'"

They sat there talking for a long time. People went in and out. Every time the door opened, it squeaked, and then a bell rang. Mitch told her he'd been watching her every day. "Watching you chug down the street."

"Don't tell me I chug," she cried lightheartedly.

"You chug," he said. "Your chin's out, you're walking fast, and anyone can tell you are one person who knows exactly where she's going . . . in every sense of the word."

"Oh, well . . ." She laughed. "No, I wouldn't say that about me."

"I would," he said confidently.

It was nearly dark when they left the sandwich shop, and as she walked next to Mitch, Nina saw everything around her—the massed lines of cars and buses, the cyclists and joggers—with a sudden, intense pleasure. Light spilled from stores and buildings. Students hurried home. The air was fresh, crisp, and it occurred to Nina that October was probably one of her favorite months.

Then something extraordinary happened. Mitch began to talk about October as if everything in her head had only been part of a conversation they were having. "October always makes me feel strange. Probably because I did something not so good one year in October."

"What was that?"

"Well—" He took her hand. "I was fifteen, and it

was right around the time my parents got separated. Looking back now, it's easy to see that was what was heating me up. But then, at that time, I thought I didn't even care that much. My sister, Trissy, was a mess over it. I was Mr. Cool." He laughed. "So cool, I stole my father's car. Anyway, the police called it stealing. I sure didn't think of it that way. For me, it was just— Ha! Something to do. You know how kids are. I skipped school one day, beautiful October day, couldn't stand those walls around me, and I walked up to the university, where Dad worked. He never locked his car, always kept the key in the ashtray. So I got in and drove it away. Ten minutes afterward, he reported it stolen. The police picked me up about an hour later and took me to a detention home for kids."

"Oh, how awful!"

"It was pretty bad," he said. "I've noticed I get sort of depressed every year just around that time."

"Now?" Nina asked.

"No, I'm not depressed *now*," he said. "But at the beginning of the month, before I went on this job, I was in a slump." They stood outside her building. "Let's go out tonight, Nina. Let's go for a walk or to a movie, whatever you want. I don't live very far away, practically just around the corner."

"I have a lot of work to do tonight," she said. "A paper for my lit course, and I should read sixty pages in my psych book—"

"Oh. A paper to write. Just one?" Mitch groaned. "That was one of the things I couldn't take about college. Continually being told what to do—and when —by other people."

"Oh, I don't mind," Nina said. "I don't look at it that way."

"Well, what's a good night for you?" he asked.

"I try not to go out too much during the week. If I let even a day go by without working, it seems I fall so far behind—"

"Friday night, then? You don't study all the time."

"Friday night would be good," she said. Then all at once she changed her mind. She didn't want to wait until Friday to see him and be with him again. And she thought that if she went straight up to the apartment, skipped supper and got to work, she could meet him around ten o'clock. But then she changed her mind again—she didn't want to be too eager—and said, "What about Wednesday?"

"Great!" he said, and he went away with a brimming smile that stayed with her for the rest of the day.

Chapter Three

"You're going to wear jeans?" Sonia said. "That's it? Your first date with the guy, and you're going to wear jeans, Nina? And no makeup?"

Sonia sounded so shocked that Nina had to smile. "I never wear makeup."

"I've noticed," Sonia said with a little sniff. "But how about it? Break out! A little mascara at least. Your eyes could use it."

Nina stared at herself in the mirror. Her eyes were sore. Did they look red and horrible? She had stayed up till three o'clock the night before, drinking coffee while she worked on her paper for Professor Lehman. She had written it twice, and gone over every word, every comma and question mark. She thought she hadn't forgotten anything, and then, this afternoon, a moment after she had put the paper on his desk, she realized she'd made a serious mistake. She had written about the mother and her daughter Emily in the story, but had forgotten all about the symbolism. The symbolism! Professor Lehman was always talking about symbols. As if forgetting the symbols wasn't bad enough, she was worried that she had put in too much personal stuff.

Whenever she did a paper she worried, but not just her ordinary, everyday, am-I-understanding-enough, am-I-doing-this-right sort of worrying. She worried more, and this was because of her secret idea that someday maybe she'd be a writer. She was majoring in Early Childhood Education; she liked kids a lot: would probably become a teacher. That was her "real-life" goal. But then, in the back of the back of her mind, there was this other idea. It had first appeared in tenth grade, when she wrote an English comp about her father's heart surgery. Mrs. Abrahams had raved about the part where Nina told how her father picked up his pajama top to show everyone who came into the house his scar. Afterward Nina was ashamed that she had revealed such private family details, and she tore up the composition. Despite that she had never forgotten the things Mrs. Abrahams had said about it. "You should really try out for the newspaper, Nina. Real talent shown here!" For a variety of reasons Nina hadn't taken Mrs. Abrahams' advice, but a seed had been sown. Ever since, Nina had had this secret thought in the back of her mind, _Someday . . . someday, I'll write a book . . . or a story. . . ._

She had hung around after class, hoping to get up

the nerve to ask Professor Lehman if she could take her paper back. But instead, when he looked inquiringly at her, she had gotten cold feet and told him she was looking for typing work. Which was true, but not the point. And then he had said he would "keep her in mind," which translated, Nina thought, into *Not interested, thanks.*

As a result of all that, plus Sonia's fussing, Nina's frame of mind was not the best when she went out to meet Mitch. She had put on a pretty blouse and tied ribbons on the ends of her braids, but was sure she didn't look "feminine" enough. Her mental image of herself was not flattering: too short, too sturdy; clumsy and snorting air through her mouth like an asthmatic dog.

Mitch was just coming up the street, and she was taken aback to see him looking entirely different in a dark shirt open at the neck to show a gold chain with a turquoise ornament. Where was "the painter"? He looked, instead, like a *painting.* Portrait of a Young Man with Turquoise Ornament. He looked, in fact, beautiful.

"Hello, Nina," he said.

"Hello, Mitch." Looking down she was anguished to see that she had forgotten to change her tattered sneakers.

"What would you like to do?" he said as they set off down the street.

"Anything you'd like to do," she said quickly.

"Well, I'd like to do something you'd like to do. How about bowling? Do you like to bowl?"

"That would be fine, but I'm not very good at it."

"Maybe a movie, then. Do you know what's playing?"

"No, do you?"

"I have a feeling that the last time I looked, there wasn't anything worth seeing." She thought he sounded subdued. Was he disappointed in her? Was it their clothes? The formality of a "date"? The ease of their first meeting certainly seemed altogether gone.

"Want something to eat?" he asked.

"I just ate."

"I thought we could get something to eat," he said gloomily.

Everything she said was wrong. It was like taking a test and being unable to stop yourself from filling in every blank incorrectly. You know you're getting everything wrong, but you can't figure out how to do it right, and on you go, writing in wrong answer after wrong answer, knowing the only outcome is failure.

"*I'm hungry,*" he said. And he sounded, she thought, nearly ready to cry, like one of her little brothers bawling, "I'm hungry, I'm hungry, doesn't anybody *care*?"

"Let's go get something, then," she said contritely.

"I don't want to eat if you're not going to."

"But that's silly," she said in a coaxing voice. "You're hungry; that's no good. Anyway, I'll have something, too," she added, and her breath came easier, she ventured a smile, wanted to pat his hand reassuringly. Maybe everything was going wrong only because he was hungry?

They went into a diner and sat down. Mitch wolfed

down his food, eating for a few minutes without speaking. "I guess you were hungry," Nina said.

"I didn't have anything in my place except eggs."

"Don't you like eggs?"

"They're all right, but I've eaten eggs just about every night this week. I got sick of them."

"Omelets are nice. My specialty is a cheese omelet." She couldn't believe they were talking about eggs. The other day in the sandwich shop it seemed they couldn't crowd in everything they had to say to each other. And now eggs!

When they left, they walked the length of the block in silence, until at the corner he said, "Who's Richie?"

"What?" she said, surprised.

"Richie," he repeated. "Who's Richie?"

"My brother. Is that what you mean? My brother? Why do you want to know about my brother?"

"Richie's your brother? The one on your raincoat?"

She nodded. "It used to be his slicker. I took it when he went away."

"Oh!" He laughed suddenly, put his arm through hers, and drew her close, saying, "I thought he was competition."

"No," she said, and she began to smile, also.

"I thought maybe he was your boyfriend."

"No," she said again. "How about you? I mean, do you have a girl friend?"

"I don't have anyone."

"Are you sure?"

"Sure, I'm sure."

"You wouldn't just say that?"

"No, Nina. I'm not that sort of person."

"Well, I know, it's just that I know this girl—" she didn't want to say Lynell's name "—and the guy she's going with didn't exactly lie to her, but he didn't tell her the truth, either, about this other girl he was going with."

"Was that you?"

"No," she said, smothering a laugh. "Not me."

"I wouldn't do anything like that to a girl," he said.

"I know it. I really know that."

"Do you? How do you know that?"

"You're a nice guy."

"I am?"

"Aren't you?"

"You said it, so I must be."

They were both enjoying this. The strain of the first hour had disappeared. They swung hands. He was at least two inches taller than she, and she liked the way he glanced down at her, brown eyes full of a radiant softness.

"What else do you know about me?" he asked.

"Not very much."

"Oh, come on, you were doing so well."

She shook her head, smiling, but said, "You're easy to be with."

"That's good. And you—you're wonderful to be with." Then in a serious voice, "Nina, I'm nearly in love with you already."

She didn't know what to say. Startled, dazed, she stared at the turquoise ornament on his chest, wondering if he was chilly without a jacket. No one had ever made such a declaration to her, and she took it in thirstily, as if she'd been waiting all her life for it. Mitch linked his hand to hers. Was he waiting for her to speak? Her lips had gone dry and rough; she hoped he wouldn't mind when they kissed.

"I'm not a virgin," she said. Her face became hot with misery. Why had she said that?

"Well, neither am I."

Then she was even more miserable. How many girls had he slept with? Each one must have been beautiful and far more clever than she could ever hope to be.

"What's the matter?" he said. "Is something wrong?"

"I hardly know you," she said in a muffled voice. She yanked off the ribbons on her braids. Why had she braided her hair? Childish!

"The feeling is what counts," he said softly. "Not time. I had a feeling about you from the first time I saw you coming down the street. Do you have any feeling for me?" Each time he said *feeling* he squeezed her hand. He began to talk about himself, saying that he was lonely, he had never had a serious relationship with a girl, and that although they were both young, he sensed she, too, had thought about life.

"I didn't leave school on a lark," he said. "I don't want you to think I'm irresponsible. I put in two years. Those two years were for my parents. I promised them that, and I did it, but I felt cut off from the real world. No one else on planet Earth lives the way we Americans do. People everywhere else are so much poorer! The rules of the games are rougher, everything is closer to the bone, and it's often a question of Are we gonna survive, not Can we get a new TV or another Pac-Man game!"

She nodded. Survival—she understood that. Her family had never been bone poor, but everything had become more difficult after her father's operation. They lived on his disability and what her mother earned. Not too much.

"What bothers me," Mitch said, "is the thought, Can I survive in the real world? The world where people don't have everything handed to them. I'm finding out. I'm testing myself. I'm learning things, Nina: how to work, how to take care of myself. I'm finding my strengths," he said so earnestly that her dream, her first dream about him, floated through her mind. Not the dream, exactly, but the tenderness of her feelings for him and the way she had put her hand on his arm.

On a dark corner she stood up on her toes, gripped his shoulders and kissed him. They wrapped their arms around each other and kissed for a long time. Nina became light-headed and thought of the Chagall paintings she'd seen by chance in the library. Women in drifting wedding gowns, and dogs, and violins, all floating in blue-green skies. They kissed and kissed and Nina floated in a blue-green sky.

"Nina." Mitch said her name in that caressing way. Neenah. They moved even closer to each other.

✢   ✢   ✢

Nina Bloom

Some Thoughts About "I Stand Here Ironing"

I liked "I Stand Here Ironing," the short story by Tillie Olsen. I could understand the story very well. The mother is worried about her daughter Emily. She thinks that she made a lot of mistakes in the past with Emily, who is nineteen years old now. It seems that Emily is in some kind of trouble, but the reader never finds out what the trouble is. For one thing, Emily is probably still feeling bad that when she was seven and sick her mother had to put her in a home. Something like that would make a child extremely upset. I know because things happened to me when I was younger that upset me, even though I was always with my parents. I was very upset, for instance, the year my father had his open heart surgery—and I was a lot older than Emily. (I didn't know if my father was going to live. He did, but he was not like his old self at all.)

At the beginning of the story the mother is ironing, and she's ironing at the end of the story. Nothing really happens, but we find out about her life and we understand why she made mistakes. It's very believable. She was alone, and she was poor, and she had children to care for.

But the ending is terrible! The mother

compares Emily to a <u>dress</u> under the iron.
And she says, "Let her be. So all that is in
her will not bloom, but in how many does
it? . . . Only help her to know . . . that she
is more than this dress on the ironing
board, helpless before the iron."

I think that this means that the iron is
like all the terrible things that happen in
life to people. It frightened me to think
of a person like that dress, flat on the ironing board, being run over by the hot iron.
Too bad that Tillie Olsen, who is really a
wonderful writer, ended the story this way.
I could see the dress on the clothesline, too,
sort of waving in the wind, full of air. That
would give a more hopeful feeling to the
story. But maybe it wouldn't be true
enough. Maybe the mother <u>couldn't</u> see that
Emily's life could change, because <u>hers</u>
never had. She still had little children to
care for, and no money and no time. So
she felt hopeless, and that is why she felt
hopeless about her daughter.

The mother felt that things in life just
<u>happen</u> to people. That is true sometimes,
such as my father's heart trouble. But still
I think people should try not to be de-
feated. Maybe Emily will be the sort of
person who won't be flattened like the
dress. Her mother can't help her anymore,
but maybe Emily will help herself.

Nice, direct approach, Miss Bloom. You understood the story well. The analogy at the end, of the iron to fate, the dress to the person, is all-important and powerful. Notice how the iron, introduced as a concrete detail, takes on weight and meaning and becomes a symbol by the end of the story. Keep trying to understand what you read.

N.L.

Chapter Four

"Pardon my French, but you're an idiot," Sonia said amiably as Nina hung half asleep over a glass of orange juice.

"Mmm?" Nothing bothered Nina. Call her an idiot. Call her a moron. Insults slid off her skin. She was armored, wrapped in a shining shield. Love. Mitch. Ah, God. She sighed, smiled muzzily into her juice, then yawned so hard, her ears cracked.

"Let's stay up all night," Mitch had said late last night when they'd stopped for something to eat.

"We could have breakfast together," Nina said.

"I wouldn't go to work. We'd both play hookey."

"No classes for me?"

"Definitely not! We'd watch the sun rise, then go back to my place and sleep all day."

"Then stay up all night again," Nina said. "And sleep all day."

"We'll never appear in daylight again. Our skin will turn white. We'll grow fangs and live on nothing but blood and white worms."

Hours later, leaning against each other, they'd gone up the stairs in The Lion's Arms, sleepily nuzzling and kissing. Behind the door, Nina heard Emmett scratching. "Poor Emmett. He feels neglected. He looks at me like, What the devil is going on, Nina? I run in, feed him, and run out. He's used to lots more attention than that. Okay, Emmett," she called softly. It was so late that even the guys on the floor below, who played reggae half the night, were quiet. "I should go in now," she said.

"And I should leave." The next moment they began kissing again.

Every night for a week she had gone to sleep thinking about Mitch, and awakened in the morning with his name in her head. She was in love. Loved him. Loved everything about him. Easy to love his eyes: deep, soft-brown, big eyes; dark irises; long, dark, deep eyelashes. And his hair: curly, thick, glossy, beautiful hair. "Mitch has beautiful hair," she said to Sonia, just to say his name. She loved his hands, too, even the calluses on the base of his thumb. Loved his long, bony, intelligent feet, and his knobby knees, and the little pad of surprising baby fat around his waist. Skinny all over except for that one secret place.

"You're making a wreck of yourself, Nina," Sonia went on, her voice lowering to a sorrowful motherliness. "Nobody can keep going on three hours sleep a night."

"You're right. You're right." Except she *was* going on three hours or four hours of sleep. Maybe she'd never need more. Love would fuel her. A modern miracle. College Girl Amazes World, Never Sleeps More Than Three Hours. Another miracle: He loved her. Miracle of miracles? Said he loved everything about her. Looked at her legs (stumpy legs which she hated) and said, *Adorable . . . love your legs, cute, solid little soldier legs. . . .*

My legs? You fool. She had laughed with gratitude, shame, pleasure.

"What time did you come in last night?" Sonia asked.

"Don't know. Three, I think." She had been coming in late night after night. Or was it morning after morning? She yawned again, and her eyes teared.

"Hon, you look like death warmed over."

"Don't tell me, please!"

Sonia herself looked fresh and rosy as she chewed an English muffin with appetite. "Lynell, wait, wait, I'm almost ready," she called.

A short while later, avoiding herself in the mirror, Nina pulled a comb through her hair and went out with knapsack slung hurriedly over her shoulder. The scaffold was gone: Mitch had finished the job two days ago. And now the house next door bloomed raspberry in the gray morning. What if she hadn't gone into the sandwich shop that afternoon? Hadn't met him? Had let it all slip through her fingers? Impossible thought. Didn't everything happen the way it had to happen?

Moving with less than her usual briskness through the tide of students, she thought that Sonia was right. She should really come in earlier, get a little more sleep. It was murderous trying to stay awake and alert all day on so little sleep. Later that day in the Poli Sci lecture hall she fell asleep sitting up, her chin propped in her hand, but only for a minute or so, and no one noticed.

The night before, she and Mitch had talked about going to an early movie, but then, instead, they had done exactly what they'd done on their first night and nearly all the other nights since: walked for hours, kissing and saying, What if? What if Mitch hadn't taken that painting job (he'd had a choice)? What if she hadn't worn Richie's slicker inside out (this had given him his opening remarks to her)? What if, in fact, weeks earlier, Nina hadn't accidentally gone into the music building, seen Lynell's and Sonia's notice for a roommate? It struck them with wonder that so many details had had to fall into place for them to meet.

No, I've got to get in earlier, Nina told herself several times as the day wore on. She was tired. But later, instead of eating supper, she took a nap. And then, when she met Mitch, getting to sleep on time didn't seem all that important.

The clouded sky had cleared up. It was a warm, starry night, with a faint sharp smell of burning leaves in the air. They climbed the hill in Beaumont Park to the water tower and lay on the grass, arms around each other, Mitch's sweater rolled up as a pillow. "Comfortable?" he asked.

"Mmm." She moved closer. "You?"

"Not bad. We could go back to my place."

"I know. But it's nice here."

"Not as private." There were cars parked lower down, and other couples passed now and then. "Nina . . . don't you want to make love?"

"Yes . . . but not yet."

"Why?"

"I want it to be—don't laugh—"

"I won't."

"I want it to be right. Not something we do just for the hell of it."

"It wouldn't be," he protested. "You think I'm running around screwing any girl I can get my hands on?"

"No, it's not that."

"Then what are you worried about?"

"I'm not worried, Mitch. It's just a feeling I have . . . that it's not time yet. But we'll know when it is the time. Do you think that's stupid?"

"No, it's not stupid. Don't say that about yourself. As long as you want to—because I sure do!" And after a moment he added, "You're strong. I knew you were strong the first time I saw you coming down the street. You can tell a lot from the way people walk. I knew you were connected, a person who's hooked in. You don't get confused."

She was flattered, but felt compelled to say truthfully enough, "I get confused lots of times. I'm not that clear about things. I wish I was."

"Are you clear about me?"

"Yes."

"No doubts?"

"None."

"How do you see me? Do you have an opinion about me?"

"Of course!" She sat up, wrapping her arms around her knees. "I see you as someone—wonderful. You think about things. You have high ideals. You have principles. When you believe in something, you believe in it all the way."

"My God! Where did you get all those ideas about me?"

"From the way you walk. You can tell a _lot_ from the way someone walks."

"I'll get you for that." He bear-hugged her until she screamed, then released her and lay back with a smug smile. "Now tell me about my high principles and ideals."

"Well, look at the way you left college," she said, still a little breathless. Her cheeks were burning. "When you told me, I first thought, Now, why didn't Mitch go to school part-time and get a job part-time? That's what I would have done. I mean, my mind works in a very practical way. But then I realized, No, that isn't the way you are. When you get an idea, when you think something is right, you go for it all the way. And I admire that."

"How do you know it wasn't cowardice? Maybe I was failing in school and ducking out to avoid all my problems."

"You were probably very smart in school."

"Not that smart."

"I bet you were always on the honor roll in high school."

"Does it show that much?"

"So you weren't failing in college, were you?" she pressed.

"My marks were okay. It wasn't the studying I couldn't handle. It was thinking that I was avoiding real life. I've been sheltered and taken care of all my life, and there I was, going on twenty-one and still being sheltered."

Nina stared at him in amazement. She didn't feel sheltered at all; on the contrary, for her, being in college reminded her of nothing so much as the time her father had thrown her into the water and told her to swim. She'd learned, but it hadn't been easy. "Who said it would be?" her father had asked. "Is your family mad at you for quitting school?" she said.

"Not mad exactly. More . . . disappointed. My father's pretty certain it was a stupid thing to do. My mother doesn't get mad at me, even when she should, but I know she wishes I'd go back to school. And what about you, Nina? Does it bother you that I'm a dropout? Because I know school is important to you."

She hugged him and rubbed her nose against his. "My own little dropout."

"You make me sound like a cookie."

"A chocolate chip dropout." The silliness stifled an impulse to say, *Yes, it does bother me a little that you're a dropout*. She thought it unworthy of her love to be doubtful about anything Mitch was, did, or said. She was going to get her degree, though. Nothing was going to stand in the way of that. "We're very different. You think first, and then you act on your beliefs and what you've figured out. Whereas I don't know if I even have beliefs, as such."

"Sure you do. Everybody does. Everybody thinks about things."

Nina shook her head. "No, I go by my feelings. . . . It's not the same. I know the way I am. I want something and . . . I *want* it. Or I get mad about something —that's why I'm in college. I didn't think that through. It doesn't make me proud. I just got mad at Mr. P., didn't want him to put me down. I don't admire myself for that."

"You're wrong not to value your instincts," he said. "That's really what you're talking about. Instincts. Spontaneity. That's what I meant when I said you were in touch, connected."

Above them the stars burned in the sky. From below rose the sounds of cars and a dog barking. It wasn't safe to stay in the park too late. Soon, Nina knew, they'd get up, find someplace to eat, maybe go to Mitch's place for a while.

They kissed for a long time. Almost in a dream, Nina remembered a moment, years ago, when she'd seen her mother playing with her baby brother, swinging him into the air, her face shining and a look so pure in her eyes that the little Nina had wanted to cry out in anguish.

"Mitch, I love you," she said against his lips. Had she been looking for someone to love—and in turn to love her—in that purehearted way ever since that day she'd seen her mother swinging her baby brother? She hadn't even known she was searching, and yet now, hadn't she found what she wanted and needed in Mitch?

A few nights later, in Mitch's apartment, they made love. It didn't go well. Nina blamed herself; did it mean that she was not a warm, sexual person? It couldn't be Mitch. She had tried to act joyous and ecstatic throughout, but in truth, whatever was supposed to happen hadn't happened for her. And afterward, instead of being exultant, she was only conscious of her shoulders aching.

"Not so good, huh?" Mitch said sadly.

"I'm sorry . . . I guess I was kind of tense. I don't know why."

"Maybe I don't know what to do so well," he said. "I mean, for the girl and—"

"No, no, I'm such a dope. I don't know anything," she wailed. And despite herself, the tears came. She sniffled angrily and wiped her eyes on the sheet.

"Don't cry, honey." He held her. "You were wonderful. It's not you. I'm not that smart about this. I haven't—you know—had that much experience. . . ."

"You haven't? But I thought—"

"No."

"I haven't, either. I mean, the one time—it hardly counts."

"One time? But *I* thought—"

"One time," she said, half angrily, half sniffling. "One time. One time!"

"Geez," he said, and looking at each other, they began laughing.

Chapter Five

Skeleton cutouts hung in the windows and crinkly orange and black crepe paper was draped over lamps and doorways. "Why are you washing dishes?" Nina said, poking her head into the kitchen.

Sonia turned. "Isn't it disgusting? As soon as I get around D.G., I go all domestic."

"Want a sip?" Nina held a paper cup of wine to Sonia's lips. Mitch hadn't come to the Halloween party thrown by D.G. and his roommates. "No, thanks, Nins," he'd said. "Hanging out with that crowd? No thanks. But if you want to go—"

"What crowd? What do you mean? You liked Sonia when you met her."

"I don't mean Sonia, hon. It was her friend D.G. I didn't warm up to."

"He's really a sweet guy, Mitch. I know he's a little stuffy, but—"

"What bothers me about D.G. is that he's such a typical business school type. He'll definitely be a corporate executive, a vice president in charge of—of *something*. He's already got the initials to go with the job."

One evening Nina and Mitch had met Sonia, D.G., Lynell, and Adam to drink beer and talk. Nina had had high hopes that they would like Mitch, and that he would like them.

"Did you hear what he said his ambition is? To make a million before he's thirty. Only he says, 'a mil.' 'I'm going to make a mil before I'm thirty.' Come on, now! Is that all there is to life? And what if he doesn't make his mil? Does that mean he's a, quote, Failure, unquote?"

Not answering, Nina had rubbed the back of Mitch's neck. Why so vehement about D.G.? Possibly because making money was what Mitch's family wanted him to do?

At first Nina thought she wouldn't go to the party, either. It wouldn't be any fun without Mitch. But then, in one of those conversations Lynell and Sonia were always carrying on, Lynell had referred to her and Mitch as "the Siamese twins."

"I heard that, Lynell," Nina had called from the kitchen where, much to his distress, she was rubbing flea powder into Emmett's fur.

Lynell appeared in the doorway. "Good. So I can ask you something I really want to know. Don't you two guys ever get sick of hanging out together?"

Did that mean she and beautiful Adam did? "No, never," Nina said, and laughed heartlessly with pleasure. But later she decided she ought to go to the party alone. A little demonstration of independence. She'd go, and she'd have a damn good time!

"So Mitch really isn't going to show?" Sonia said, hanging up the dishcloth.

"Nope. I'm on my own tonight."

"Know what Lynell calls you two?" Sonia's lips were painted a vivid red, her eyes outlined in mascara. "The Siamese—"

"I know," Nina said, cutting her off.

"Well, don't take it to heart. And don't tell Lynell I said so, but maybe she's a little, little bit jealous."

"Oh, come on!" Nina smiled disbelievingly. "Lynell jealous of me?"

"Not you, exactly. You and Mitch."

"Well, why? She's got Adam."

"Yes, that's the point." Sonia's eyes gleamed. "They're having their problems."

"Oh! You mean the girl back home. But I thought he was going to straighten all that out." Lynell and Adam had been having a passionate love affair for weeks before she discovered that he was also having a passionate love affair with a girl in his hometown of Flint. In his room one day she had seen a stack of blue envelopes, asked a few questions, and before she could say "Michigan," Adam was telling all. And crying. Crying and crying, and begging Lynell to give him time to get it all straight.

"He says he just hasn't been able to bring himself to break Ms. Michigan's heart by telling her about

Lynell. *Who*, he says, is the *true* love of his life."

"A real prince," Nina said, her heart rising in sympathy for Lynell. In fact, Adam did look princely. Tall, with an arched nose and an aristocratic bearing, he was one of the handsomest men Nina had ever seen. The first time she met him she had been so startled by his beauty, she had almost felt like curtsying. But there had been something else, something about his smile, a certain satisfaction, that made her wonder if, underneath his charm, he wasn't a cold fish.

"Sonia—" D.G. put his head in the door. "Oh, Nina, hi. I didn't see you come in. Glad you're here. Where's the good friend?"

"Didn't feel like partying, D.G.," Nina said. "I like your tie." For the occasion D.G. was wearing a bright orange tie striped with black. He was a large, affable-looking person with a handsome, reddish face. If he could grow a bushy mustache, Nina thought, he would look exactly like one of those blustery-but-good-hearted colonels in some old English movie.

"D.G.," she said, smiling at him, "did you say you want to be a millionaire before—"

"I'm thirty," he confirmed. *"But—"* He raised a finger. "I didn't say I *want* to be one, Nina. What I said was, *I will be*. I—"

"No, no, no, don't you dare get started on your Grand Plan." Sonia gave D.G. a shove. "Come on, baby, get me out of this kitchen."

In the living room a large-boned young woman wearing a red flannel shirt stopped D.G. "Sweetie, where's the prole you promised me?"

"He didn't come, Kath. It's Nina's boyfriend."

"Prole?" Nina said.

"Proletarian," Kath said importantly. "D.G. said your boyfriend dropped out of college."

"That's right."

"And became a worker. With his *hands*."

"Yes," Nina said.

"Well, I'm writing my master's thesis on college dropouts, and I really need case studies to illuminate my stats. I wanted to interview your boyfriend."

"Oh. Well, I'll tell him."

"Damn! I was looking forward . . . Maybe you can help. Where does his family live? What's their income status? Is he middle class, upper class, or lower class in his socioeconomic origins?"

Nina stared. Then, as the bundle of weighty words sorted themselves out, she got mad. Here she was, back with the bluebirds and the buzzards. Only now they were *upper class* and *lower class*. Lower class! The words set her teeth on edge. That was her. That was her parents, and her brothers, and her grandmother.

"I think," she said, doing what for her was a good imitation of Lynell's cool Californian tones, "Mitch was born a bluebird. But he's a buzzard now." Then she spoiled the whole effect by flushing violently.

Kath shrugged and walked away. Nina moved across the room, stopping at a table loaded with food and bottles to refill her wine cup. By the window she saw Lynell talking to Adam. The heat in her face slowly subsided, and she watched Adam with interest for some sign of suffering. But with his high broad forehead and full lips, with his perfectly unwrinkled shirt and carefully knotted tie, Adam just didn't look like a sufferer. In fact, hovering over Lynell, both hands on her arms, he seemed to be thoroughly happy. I bet, Nina thought, he enjoys having two women. And she couldn't help being swept by a glow of satisfaction that *her* man was totally unlike either the selfish Adam or the stuffy D.G.

Behind the hum of conversation was the throb of rock music. Some people were dancing, a lot more standing around, drinking and talking. It wasn't a real Halloween party, not the kind she remembered as a kid, where they dunked for apples and played tricks in dark rooms. Not that she would have wanted a kids' party! Still, after another cup of wine, a nostalgic glow for the good old Halloween parties enveloped her as she drifted around, listening to people talk.

"He was awfully darling," a girl in a striped jump suit said as Nina passed. "Everybody loved him. Me, too! But I decided not to let him know. I didn't want to make his ego any bigger! Soooo, he thought I hated him!"

Too bad Mitch wasn't here. Was she the only single in the room? That made her feel a bit conspicuous. Did it make any sense that she'd come without him? Typical of her to do something like that on impulse. If she'd thought about it a bit more . . . Really, what difference did it make what Lynell thought about her and Mitch? Well, she was here now, and not about to run out early and then have to listen to Lynell's little digs about her and Mitch not being able to spend two hours apart without going into shock. She finished her wine and took yet another cup. Might as well get high. It would make everything go more smoothly.

"Do you know," Nina overheard, "that there's a column now like Dear Abby, only especially for people living together? They call it *Hello, LTers*. . . . Cute!"

"So I told him making love would definitely wreck our relationship . . ."

"No, no, overnight *she* changed. She was this terrific person, and then she got married, and suddenly she was Mrs. Bullshit. . . ."

Was everyone talking about love and sex? Or was that all she picked up on her radar?

More wine. Eavesdropping was fun. She hoped she could remember everything to tell Mitch and make him laugh.

She sat down on the floor next to another girl who also seemed to be alone. "Hi, I'm Nina. I'm a friend of D.G.'s."

"I'm Sari. I'm a friend of Jake's."

"Don't know Jake, Sari."

"He's one of the roommates. See him over there?" She pointed to a big, bearded bear of a man. "That's Jake, a super person."

Nina gave Sari a dreamy smile. "Love your hair. It's gorgeous."

"I haven't cut it in fifteen years." Sari's hair hung in two thick braids down to her waist. "I woke up sad this morning, then I thought about my hair, and it made me feel better. I'll never cut it. What'd you say your name was—Tina?"

"Nina."

"Right. Are you here with someone?"

"No, my boyfriend stayed home."

"Are you living with him? I live with Steve. See him over there." She pointed again to an intense-looking blond.

"Cute," Nina said appreciatively.

"I know, he's a darling. His main fault is he's into engagements. Is your boyfriend into engagements? I don't want to be tied down. Do you? Marriage is so end-of-the-line." She leaned toward Nina. "I'll tell you something else, Gina—"

"Nina," Nina said politely.

"Kevin Porter lives with Kath Colson now—"

"Kath, who's doing her master's thesis?"

"Right. Big Kath. But last year Kevin Colson and I were living together. How-ever, not for long. I said, No thanks, bye-bye, you're not my type. Fair enough, right? I got another guy, he's got another girl. But everywhere I go these days, there he is—my ex. Do you think he follows me around? Do you think he's giving me a message? I won't talk to him. I refuse. If he asks what we're talking about, you tell him I said, 'Forget it, Kevin, we are a thing of the past.'"

Nina hugged her knees, smiling out of her wine glow. What a funny, funny, weird conversation. If only Mitch were here; they would look at each other and . . . No, no, better that he wasn't here; they would never be able to control their faces.

"Dance, Nina?" It was D.G., standing, red-faced, over her.

Nina stood up. Her head spun, and she held on to D.G.'s arm. "Great talking to you, Tina," Sari said.

"You, too, Mary."

"I think her name is Sari," D.G. said as they started dancing.

"Oh, really?" Nina said innocently. "Did I tell you I like your Halloween tie, D.G.?"

"Yes, you did, Nina. And I like your dress. I really dig it."

It was a Pakistani dress, a soft purple, long and loose, that she'd bought a few weeks ago at the Thrift Shop Boutique.

"And I also like your button," she said, leaning close to read it. On the pocket of his shirt was pinned a green button that said, KISS ME, I AM COSMIC. "What does it mean?"

"I don't know. Sonia gave it to me." The music changed to a slow beat, and D.G. pulled Nina closer. "You know, Nina, you're very Mother Earth. I would just like to lie down somewhere with you. We could be cosmic together."

"D.G., you dog!"

"Now don't tell Sonia I said that. I'm just being truthful. I'm very attracted to you."

"Well, I—uh, thanks." She thought her face must be as red as his.

The music stopped. D.G. squeezed her hand and said he better go find Sonia. Nina wandered around the room and danced with a boy with a mole on his cheek who told her she had substantial vibrations.

"Do you think I'm very Mother Earth?" she asked. She couldn't stop smiling. Everything was vivid. She saw *this . . . that . . . this . . . that . . .* snatches of color and sound. . . .

The room was hot. Nina pulled her dress out from her body and moved around, smiling at everyone. Nice people. Blessings on them. I, Nina, bless you one and all. In the kitchen D.G. and Sonia were wrapped together in a long kiss. "Ooops." Nina backed out. They're being cosmic together, she thought wisely.

Oh, good. She was dancing again with the boy with the mole on his cheek. He hugged her. "I lu-uuuve parties," Nina said. Wine again in the clever little paper cups with the clever little handles.

The boy with the mole followed her around the room. And now D.G. was out of the kitchen and reading the stock market report out loud. "Boo! Hiss!"

"Shut up, D.G."

"Price of steel rose point o—"

"Sonia! Where's Sonia? Sonia, shut him up, Sonia."

"No, leave D.G. alone," Nina said. "Everybody should do what makes them happy." How profound. She hugged a girl. "Are you happy, dear?" She climbed on a chair. "Everyone. Listen. I luu-uuuuuuuuve Mitch."

His name brought tears to her eyes. Mitch! Poor Mitchell! Home all, all, all alone! She had left him all, all, all alone for hours and hours and *hours*. She had left him all, all, all alone while *she* was at a party having a wonderful time.

"Selfish," she muttered, finding her coat. "Sel-*fish*!"

Outside, she scuffed leaves. Cold air. A smoky moon. "The moon in June," she sang. Was she high? A bit. She stumbled. Yes, a teensy-weensy bit high. She held out her arms, rocked along. Wonderful party. Won-

derful friends. Sonia. Lynell. D.G. *Wonderful* friends.
Adam, too. Prince Adam. Wonderful, wonderful
friends. True buddies of the heart. "The moon in
June . . ." A car slowed down, the horn honked.
"Hello, honey."

Girls weren't supposed to walk the streets alone at
night. Advice of everyone. Do not walk streets late at
night. Phooey! She shook her fist at the car. "Bug off!
You're invading my space."

The car passed. She stared after it. Amazing. *A*-maz-
ing. *She* was amazing.

What lungs. "Bug off!" she roared to the empty
street.

"Nina, you're drunk as a skunk," Mitch said.

Nina stood with dignity in the middle of the room.
"I admit I am a teensy-weensy bit high. I admit I had
a little wine."

"A little wine does this to you?" He laughed. "Give
me your jacket, hon." He pressed her into a chair.

"Were you lonely?" she said, jumping up. "Was it
awful being all, all, all alone? I'll never leave you
alone again." She sat down on the mattress. "Does my
breath smell, Mitchell? Do I smell like a wino? Am I
too fat? Do you like Lynell? She's beautiful, beautiful.
Could be a model."

"Not my type," he said, lying down next to her.
"Too skinny."

"Mitch, Mr. Mole said I had substantial vibrations.
D.G. said I was Mother Earth." She covered Mitch's
face with kisses. "I told him, I luuu-uuuuve Mitch. I

told everybody. I told them all. I luuu-uuuuve Mitch. You are the best. You are—"

She fell asleep in midsentence and didn't wake until the next morning. It was the first time she'd slept over at Mitch's place.

Chapter Six

"You're not really going to take it?" Nina said incredulously, caught between laughter and a sneaky desire to grab Mitch's arm and hustle him on down the street.

"Nina, it's superb. Look at those lines."

She snorted, moving back a step from the old brown velvet armchair that was lying on its side on the edge of the gutter. Springs stuck out from the bottom, and in back the upholstery had a deep gash.

Mitch stroked the carved wooden arms. "You don't see stuff like this around anymore, hon. It's a find." He smacked the pillow. "Not even very dusty."

"Babyface. It's someone else's trash. My mother threw away a chair like that years ago."

"Maybe it's the same one. Grab the legs, Nina, okay?"

"You're serious!"

"I'm always serious. I'll take the back, so I get the weight on me. Lift." They moved down the street.

"How're you doing?" Mitch asked as they went up the stairs to his apartment.

"Don't ask!"

"You're out of shape, cream puff."

"Yesterday you said I was perfect."

"You are, you are. Just don't get a job with a moving company."

Later, after beating the dust out of the chair, they sat in it together and ate Mallomars, licking the chocolate from each other's fingers.

On Friday that week they shopped together, buying cheese and grapes, bread, and tins of tuna fish, and cat food for Emmett. In the checkout line they stood behind an Asian couple, both wearing pale-yellow V-necked sweaters; both small, with delicate features and dark, shining hair. They weren't holding hands or even standing especially close, but Nina whispered to Mitch, "They belong together."

"The sweaters are the give-away," he whispered back.

Nina shook her head. No, she would have known even if they hadn't been wearing matching yellow sweaters. There was something about the space they occupied, something beyond clothes or words. An aura that was almost visible, a *coupleness* that drew Nina's eyes. She imagined them going home, taking out their package of bean sprouts, their four tangerines, their long stalk of bok choy, and quietly putting everything away. They would hardly speak, but in every gesture, in every glance that passed between them, would be an acknowledgment of their connection. She moved closer to Mitch.

Over the weekend they played basketball in the park, Nina in gray sweats, Mitch with a bandanna tied around his forehead. The wind was strong, and they ran around yelling and shooting baskets, their hands becoming red and chapped. "Watch this!" Mitch threw the ball, a little awkwardly, off balance. The ball bounced off the rim. Nina caught it and laid it up neatly.

Mitch, fancy, danced the ball around in a circle, pivoted, again somewhat awkwardly, and missed again. And again Nina put the ball through the hoop. She had played with her brothers for years, the hoop fastened over their garage door.

"What is this?" Mitch said after she made a third basket.

"I'm wearing my lucky shoelaces."

In Mitch's apartment, later, they ate cheese and tomato sandwiches and listened to music. His "apartment" was, in fact, just one big room, plus a minuscule kitchen. On the floor under the front windows was his bed, a mattress with an Indian print blanket thrown over it. An old oak library table with two big drawers stood against one wall—he used it for reading and eating—the velvet armchair was in a corner, looking a little seedy; and over the library table, shelves Mitch had built were packed with his books and records.

"I'm leaving early today," Nina said. "I give you fair warning. I really have to get some studying done."

"What's early?"

"Fourish."

Mitch grinned. "That's about right."

"P.M., buster, not A.M."

"Study here. I won't bother you."

"Ha! to that. You're incapable of keeping your hands to yourself."

"You're a fine one to talk. You never leave me alone. I'm in constant danger of being molested by you."

"That's true."

Their lovemaking was better: they were both more relaxed (they even tried to read *The Joy of Sex* together, but Nina admitted it embarrassed her); they had become altogether less tense and solemn about the whole business and could laugh when things went not as expected.

Not only had Nina begun to enjoy making love, she was also glad in a general sense that she was now doing what everyone else (or so it seemed) had been doing for years. She was nearly twenty and had been uncomfortably aware of what she thought of as her *backwardness*. Her country mouseness. But now, at least, when Sonia and Lynell made certain little remarks or jokes, she knew what was meant and could even put in a word or two of her own.

In the middle of the afternoon she fell asleep curled up on the bed, clutching a pillow to her stomach.

"It's these late hours," she said on waking up, as if in answer to a question. Outside the sky had darkened. Rain spattered the windows. "I've got to get on a better schedule, Mitch, do better. . . . Maybe only stay out late on weekends or something. What do you think?"

"Sure," he said, putting a finger in his book.

"What're you reading?" She pulled the blanket around her, yawning.

"A book on European architecture. If I ever go back to school, I think it would be for architecture. Buildings and cities fascinate me. If you could live in any city in the world, which one would it be?"

"I never thought about it."

"I think about that all the time."

"Well, which one would you live in?"

"I don't know yet. I've got to visit them all first."

"You could paint houses in every city in the world."

"Not such a bad idea. Hey, I really like that."

Nina stretched pleasurably. A fine moment. The rain, the music, herself curled under the warmth of the blanket, Mitch sitting opposite her, his voice warm and dreaming. Perfect, she thought, perfect.

She must have dozed off again. He was kneeling over her. "Going to let me come in with you?"

She blinked, then looked at his watch. "Mitch, look at the time!" Outside it was dark.

"Don't go yet, Nins. I don't want you to go."

"No, I told you . . ." She got up, put on her sneakers, combed her hair. "I promised myself I'd study today." She looked around for her scarf, jacket, keys.

"Wait, wait . . . listen to this song. I want you to hear this one song." He dropped a record on the turntable and Janis Joplin's husky, sensuous voice spilled into the room. "Isn't that great?"

"Mitch— See you tomorrow?" Nina went to the door.

"*Nina.* You can wait till the song is over."

"Come on, don't do that to me."

"What? Do what?" There was an obstinate expression on his face.

"*What?* You're doing a number on me!" She walked out, slamming the door. By the time she got to the last flight of stairs, she was remorseful. Did she have to blow up? Did she have to be so impatient? She could have waited another two minutes, listened to the song. Her big failing—one of them, anyway. Once she got an idea in her head, it seemed as if nothing could dislodge it. Said she was going to leave, so she had to leave. No flexibility. Okay if the idea was right: like wanting to go to college, or living off campus, or getting together with Mitch. But the other side of that stubbornness, of deciding on a path and following it without bending, was that, one of these days, she was going to follow the wrong path. Come up against something she couldn't crash through. Not just stub her toe, but bang her head. Hard. Get herself into a mess of trouble.

Was she in trouble already—with Mitch? Halfway there. Back off, she told herself and decided that, outside, she'd call Mitch to his window, wave, smile, let him see she wasn't mad. Blow him a kiss. If she was lucky, he'd grin, make a circle of thumb and forefinger, let her know *he* wasn't mad.

But outside, looking up to his window, she was startled to find him sitting on the sill, legs dangling into space. "What are you doing?" she yelled.

"Come on back up here."

"Go inside!"

He hitched himself casually around on the sill. "Look, Ma, no hands." Nina screamed with fear and ran back up the four flights of stairs. She burst into the apartment. The window was closed. Mitch was eating an apple. "Hi," he said.

"You creep," she yelled. "You *idiot*. You could have fallen." Her heart was racing from the dash up the stairs. "You could have been killed." Crying, she pummeled him with her fists.

"Nina. Nina!" He put his arms around her, restraining her. "I didn't mean to scare you, Nina! Not like that. It was just a joke, really."

She wept stormily for a few minutes, her insides knotted, as they had been so often that year of her father's surgery. It had occurred to her that since then —or at least until she met Mitch—her life had never again been quite right. Had never been, as Mitch would say, centered. Was it because *then,* when she was fourteen, she had recognized that her father, with his thick shoulders and short powerful legs, might have died?

"Did I really scare you?" Mitch said contritely. "I'm sorry. I'm so sorry." They stood rocking together, their arms around each other. Nina didn't get back to her own place till late that night. Too late to do any real studying.

Chapter Seven

The weather turned cold, and they spent more time in Mitch's apartment. Nina brought her books with her more often and, driven by her fear of failing, gradually caught up with her backlog of work. Sometimes Mitch read while she studied, and sometimes he helped her, and sometimes he played devil's advocate to shake her up. "Horse balls," he would say to some idea she'd taken straight from her text.

"*Why?* It says right here—"

"Yes but, Nina, think. Is that what *you* really believe?"

"Why should my opinion count? The person who wrote this book—"

"I don't believe you. I don't believe you! Of course your opinion counts! What's the point of going to school if you're not going to think for yourself!"

She liked being shaken up that way, liked fighting and yelling over books.

One night, sitting on Mitch's bed, drinking cups of cocoa fuzzed with marshmallow whip, they told each other about the worst years of their lives. The awful year for Mitch had been when he was fifteen and was taken to the detention home. "I'll never forget it. I spent three days there. I was sure my parents were so mad at me, they were going to leave me there."

Nina hugged him. "I hate to even hear you talk about it. Why didn't they come get you out?"

"I don't know. They're not mean people. I guess they thought I needed to be taught a lesson. But all I was, was terrified. And I didn't really talk to my parents again for years. I told you all that. Tell me about you."

"My worst year was when I was fourteen, but compared to what happened to you—"

"That's when your father had his operation."

"Right. I used to dread going home. He'd always be in his pajamas, looking out the window. You know little girls sometimes adore their fathers? That was me. I adored him. He was Superman to me, I guess. And I'd get home and he'd be crying. Just quietly crying. I got real crazy. I think that's why I went to the cemetery with Bobby Sadler." She stopped. "Do you want to hear this?"

"If it's about you—yes."

"Well, this thing with Bobby Sadler was really strange. He was a boy in my class. I knew him from around school, the way you know a lot of kids. You just see them around, and you know their names, but it doesn't mean you ever have anything to do with them."

"What was he, a bluebird?" Mitch asked.

Nina laughed. "Bobby Sadler? No, no. But the thing was we had never even talked to each other, and then one day when I was walking home, he came driving by in his car. He had a little yellow VW with two black fenders—and he asked me, Did I want a ride? And I said, Okay. I remember thinking that if I went for a ride with him, I wouldn't have to go straight home and see my father. We drove around for a while. Didn't say a word. He was just gripping that steering wheel, staring straight ahead. And I was thinking, Well, what's going on here, Nina? And just about then Bobby said, 'Wanna go to the cemetery?'

"And I knew. So *that's* what I'm doing in this car."

"The cemetery?"

"You know. And I knew. I knew what going to the cemetery meant. But I didn't care. That's the way I was that year. I thought I didn't care about anything. And so we went there . . . and we did it. In the back seat."

After a moment Mitch said, "Why?"

"Why what?"

"Why'd you do it?"

"I told you."

"I mean, why'd you *really* do it? Some creep comes along and asks you to go to the cemetery. And you say okay. Just like that? You knew what he wanted."

"I didn't say it to myself in so many words, Mitch—"

"But you knew."

"Yes."

"Fourteen. That's too damn young." He held his cocoa cup in front of him, stiffly, not drinking.

"I didn't know that when I was fourteen. I told you what a crazy year it was for me. And besides everything else, when I look back now, I think I was curious. I remember being really afraid that I'd die and never know what sex was all about."

"Curious?" Mitch gestured, spilling cocoa. "That's a hell of a reason—curiosity!" He mopped up the cocoa with a sock, then threw it into a corner. A silence fell between them.

"Well . . . I better go." Nina got up and began dressing. Avoiding her eyes, Mitch, too, got up and pulled on his pants.

Outside it was snowing—light, stinging flakes. Nina wound her scarf around her head. "I don't know why you're so upset," she said at last.

"Oh, you're not that dumb."

"Maybe I am. Maybe I'm a lot dumber than you think. Spell it out for me."

"Can't you guess?" he said.

"The only thing I guess is . . . jealousy."

"Okay, you guessed."

"Mitch! You told me about those two girls, Shelley and Muriel. I didn't like hearing about them, but I didn't get mad at you for what you did before you met me."

"Good for you. You're a better person than I am."

"I can't believe this," Nina said quietly. "This is so ridiculous. I told you I wasn't a virgin. Remember? I told you that the first time we ever went out. Besides, it was years ago."

"Yes, but hearing all about it, every detail. Did you have to tell me every detail?" He sounded as if he were going to cry. Her heart softened. Then he slapped his hand against the wall as they went up the stairs in her building and said, "You just opened your mouth, and it all came out. Niagara Falls."

"Look, don't talk to me like that." The back of her throat burned. "I don't like your jealousy! You're unfair! *Go away!*" She pushed him, then ran to her door, key in hand.

Inside, she fell across her bed with her clothes on and was asleep at once, as hard and deep as if someone had hit her over the head.

Chapter Eight

Bent over her books as she left the library, Nina almost ran into Professor Lehman who, on this fresh cold day, wore his usual tweed jacket, but with a red wool scarf looped around his neck. "Easy," he said, steadying her. He had a racquet under one arm.

"Sorry!" Nina's face reddened. "I guess I didn't see you," she said unnecessarily. But her embarrassment turned to muted pleasure as he continued to hold her elbow.

"You're the girl who asked me about typing work. Yes? You're, ah"—he snapped his fingers—"Bloom. Miss Bloom, are you still interested in working?"

Nina nodded. "Yes, yes, I am. Very interested," she added emphatically. She needed the money, always needed money, and right now had plenty of time on her hands. Might have plenty of time on her hands for the rest of the school year. Four days since their quarrel and she still hadn't seen Mitch. Who should make the first move? She didn't think the quarrel was her fault. Let him come to her. *Niagara Falls.* A fresh wave of anger came over her. Sure she had talked. Sure she had told all. Because she *trusted* him. Did he think she went around telling her life history to *any* willing ear?

"How much work are you looking for?" Professor Lehman said. "Would a few hours a day suit you?"

"That would be perfect!"

"Do you want to come along to my office right now? Are you on your way somewhere? I can show you the work I have in mind, and you can get started tomorrow or whenever suits you."

"Now is perfect," she said again. Emphasis on *now.* Because she didn't want to go home. Didn't want to face the too-long, Mitchless evening, and Sonia's curiosity, and Lynell's half smile. (Maybe Lynell was glad to have company in her misery? She and Adam were still battling over his other girl friend. Despite that, Lynell appeared, as always to Nina, admirably cool and restrained. She, on the other hand, apparently showed everything on her face. Before she ever said a word, Sonia had guessed that she had had a fight with Mitch.)

The sun was going down behind the tall spires of the music building, spreading great fans of red, orange, and pink along the horizon. The glowing colors of the sunset seemed to spread inside Nina. Out of all his students, Nicholas Lehman had picked her to work for him. But, wait. Had he really picked her? First she had asked for the work, and now she'd almost run him down on the sidewalk. You might say she had brought herself to his attention. She gulped in a mouthful of cold air. Wanted to say something. But what could she possibly say that would interest someone like him? Trotting along at his side, silent, mute as a table, she sneaked a look at his profile. Stern, remote, devastatingly handsome.

Kim Ogun called him Lover. "He makes love to you with his eyes. I know ten girls who would give their right hands to have a chance to be alone with Nickiepie!"

"Do you play racquetball?" he asked, glancing at her.

She shook her head.

"Great game. You ought to try it."

"Oh, I will. I like games. Is it like tennis?" How naive and silly she sounded. But he smiled at her warmly.

"It's a lot faster game than tennis. You use your arm differently. Tennis is stiff-armed, whereas racquetball is a wristy game." And he demonstrated, raising the racquet, flexing his wrist.

"I see," she said brightly. They were talking. Tra-la-la, she was talking to Nickiepie.

His office was a tiny room in the basement of the Language Arts Building. A single window looked out on the sidewalk, and in the distance, a bit of sky. "Don't call it small," he said. "It's cozy." Papers and books were everywhere—covering the desk, shelves, and a green filing cabinet. Even the window ledge was stacked high with unsteady piles of books. "Make yourself comfortable." He cleared a student chair and sat down opposite her at the desk.

On the wall a bulletin board was covered with newspaper clippings, letters, and pictures. A half-page "Peanuts" cartoon in full color was bordered with green tape. "I love Peanuts," Nina said, studying the cartoon. In the first frame Sally asked Charlie Brown to help her with her homework. "You mean do it for you, don't you?" Charlie Brown said as he reclined suavely in a beanbag chair. Next, Sally leaned over his shoulder and told him, "When Leo Tolstoy was writing *War and Peace,* his wife copied it for him seven times!"

Charlie Brown got up and left the room. Sally followed, saying, "And she did it by candlelight! And with a dip pen! And sometimes she had to use a magnifying glass to make out what he had written . . . and she had to do it after their child had been put to bed and the servants had gone up to their garrets and it was quiet in the house."

Smiling, Nicholas Lehman said, "You'll understand why I put up that strip after I tell you about the article I'm planning." He took several long yellow legal pads from a drawer. "These are my notes. This is what you'll be typing for me." He loosened his tie, a gesture Nina recognized from class. "Let me tell you the background of this project," he went on. "It started a few years ago when I found an old paperback copy of some of Robert Louis Stevenson's stories in a second-hand bookstore. It was all fairly standard except for one story called 'The Body Snatchers.' A nice, ghoulish little tale about medical students who do a bit of grave-robbing. The introduction to this story mentioned that R.L.S. wrote it with his wife, Fanny Osborne. It seems that Fanny, before marrying Robert, had herself been a writer of the macabre. Well, Stevenson had recently had one of his stories turned down by an editor. Then this story he and Fanny wrote together was accepted enthusiastically by the same editor. Must have been a bit of a shock for Stevenson. When he received payment, he sent back part of the check, telling the editor the story was second-rate.

"It's true the story isn't one of his finest, but what I think was at work with him was ego. By sending back the money he was implying that had this story been pure R.L.S. it would have not been second-rate. What interested me particularly was that Fanny didn't get any credit for being cowriter."

"How unfair," Nina said.

Nicholas Lehman nodded. "Exactly. Actually, years later R.L.S. did give Fanny credit. Anyway, that story started me thinking about spouses who are, or have been, closet writers. That is, have worked in anonymous collaboration with the writer who received public credit. I wondered if Fanny and R.L.S. were an aberration. One of a kind. I've dug up numbers of cases, mostly of women, wives and sisters who have worked behind the scenes and let their husbands or brothers have the glory."

"And now you're going to write about them?"

Nicholas Lehman nodded. "I'm thinking of calling the article 'And Special Thanks to My Wife.' Or perhaps, 'Without Whose Help.' My ex-wife would appreciate this. She used to do my typing and edited everything I wrote. Once in a while she wrote a sentence or two—or three. Maybe I'm doing penance with this article for my own ego," he said, giving Nina a wry smile, as if the two of *them* understood *him* perfectly.

Dazzled—Nickiepie, indeed!—Nina gave back what she hoped was an approximation of a sophisticated smile.

"It ought to be a little different from the usual run of articles," Professor Lehman said. "At any rate, from anything I've published before. Well, what do you think, Miss Bloom?"

What did she think? She thought he was incredible. She thought she was sensationally lucky. And that this was a job like no job she'd ever had before. "It's going to be a wonderful article," she cried. Oh, God. She kept saying *wonderful* and *perfect* and whinnying like a twelve-year-old.

"I'm pleased so far. I think it'll create a bit of a stir, too. More than anything I've published previously."

"Have you written a lot of books?"

"Articles. Most of them too technical to be of interest to you."

Should she tell him her dream of someday being a writer? What would she say? Just come out with it? *Professor Lehman, someday I want to write, too.* But what if it sounded as if she were apple polishing? Maybe she should ask his advice. *Do you think I could be a writer?* How would he know? All he'd seen were a few papers she'd handed in—and gotten B's on. It wasn't even as if she were one of the outstanding students.

He pointed to a stack of magazines on a shelf. "Those are the journals I've been published in." He handed her one, and she flipped through it, reading titles. "A Celebration of George Wilde" . . . "Reality and Sanity in the Novels of Hortensia Haywood" . . . "A Second Look at Diana Askyniv's 'The Water Chorale' " . . . A vast wave of humble relief rolled over her. The moment for her to say anything about her own dream had passed, and thank God she had kept her mouth shut. Swayed by that radiant warmth in his blue eyes, she had wanted, like a puppy dog, to impress him on his own territory.

"Anything you'd like to ask now, Miss Bloom?"

She wiped her hands down the sides of her jeans. "When do you want me to start work?"

He smiled. "Not only a woman of few words, but of action. How about right now?"

Nina rolled a sheet of paper into the typewriter. It was an old machine, the keys faded, the black body covered with silver scratches. She typed a sentence or two.

"Let me see your hands," Nicholas Lehman said.

Startled, she held them out. He took hold of her fingertips. "You bite your nails. You're too old to bite your nails."

"No, I cut them with a nail clipper, that's why they're down so low." She laughed nervously. "I cut them so I won't bite them."

"Good. I don't like to see bitten fingernails."

She began typing, bending over one of the yellow

pads. "He wrote to Masters in one of those lengthy letters of his, 'Nell is looking over the pages for me and making some corrections and suggestions here and there. The brazen thing is even putting in a few additions. I must admit . . .' "

"Good. Excellent." Standing behind her, Nicholas Lehman touched Nina lightly on the shoulder. And just then, looking up, she saw through the window, low in the bit of darkening sky, an improbably romantic sliver of silver moon. And in the same moment she remembered that last night she had dreamed about Mitch. Dreamed they were in a boat, and smiling at her, he had said, "You remind me of my sister, of Trissy. And that's a compliment, Nins." "I do?" she had said. "I don't look like her at all, at all." And she woke herself up, laughing. Then, a moment later, she had realized the happiness of the dream was a lie—or a wish.

Chapter Nine

"For you." Nina thrust a little potted plant into Mitch's hand.

"Hello," he said, staring at her.

"Hello." She stared back. *Are you going to humble yourself?* Lynell had said. And Nina, edgy, had flared, *How the hell do I know, Lynell?* Humble herself? *No.* Just going to find out what the devil was happening. So maybe she'd make a fool of herself. But . . . she couldn't let this stupid quarrel go on any longer. Five days, and *nothing.* Not a call, not a word. Nothing from him, nothing from her. All week she'd been telling herself, *I have my pride.* But this morning she had awakened in a panic, thinking, *He's sick! He's had an accident!* Then she argued with herself. You're just looking for an excuse to go over there. But what if this panic meant something? What if it was like ESP, and he really was sick—and only stupid pride kept her from going to him?

"This is a surprise," he said.

"Mmmm—" She looked at him closely. He was wearing chinos and a yellow T-shirt. Bare feet. Sleepy-looking brown eyes. He sure didn't look sick. He looked, well, yummy. So good that Nina's stomach flip-flopped. And then, the way he was standing there, holding the plant she'd thrust into his hand, with a startled, almost silly expression on his face, got to her. Just got to her. Damn. It brought out the maternal in her. Made her want to hug him close, reassure him, tell him it was okay to look silly; and she loved him, *loved* him, even if he was a jealous mutt.

"Well . . . are you going to ask me in?" she said more flirtatiously than she'd intended. What she meant to do was confront him, get things out in the open, ask for straightforward answers to straightforward questions. The plant had been a last-minute impulse.

"Oh. Oh, sure! Come on in. The place is sort of—" He waved a hand. Sort of, indeed. It was a major disaster area. Clothes everywhere, bed rumpled, dirty dishes all over the table, empty wine bottle, soda cans, books, newspapers, and a bunch of other junk littering the floor. The radio was tuned to a rock station, playing loud enough, as her mother would say, to wake the dead.

Mitch looked around, set the plant down on the windowsill.

"Right, it likes light," Nina said.

"Who is this strange-looking guy, anyway? What's his name?"

"Polka-dot plant."

"*Pink* plant?"

"It's green; just the spots are pink."

"It looks diseased."

"Give it back if you don't like it!"

"Well, come on, do you have to get so mad?" He sounded uneasy. "You get mad at the drop of a hat. You know that? You know that, Nina?"

"Oh, really?" Her initial warmth fled. She eyed him coolly. Looked like he hadn't shaved all week. Probably hadn't showered, either. "Well, maybe I get mad fast, but I get over it fast, too. And I don't hold grudges," she added pointedly.

"You think I do?" He picked up a shirt, sniffed it, then stuffed it into a laundry bag hanging from a doorknob.

"What else am I supposed to think? Either that, or you don't give a damn about us. That's what I think —you *don't* give a damn. Not about me. Not about us."

"I don't know what you're talking about," he said defensively.

"Oh, sure you do. Don't, please don't come on all innocent with me. We had a fight, and I haven't seen you since then."

"You told me to go away. You said it, Nina. *Go away*."

"So *what*?"

"So I took you at your word."

"Oh, God. I don't believe this."

"I don't need that. I don't need another brush-off."

"*Another* brush-off. When did I ever—"

"Not you."

"Well, who are we talking about?"

"Look, I told you about Muriel—"

"*Muriel!*"

"Right. Muriel. I told you she . . . I told you what happened. . . ."

"She broke off with you."

"So you do remember?"

"Yes, it was a rotten deal. I don't know how you ever got mixed up with her in the first place. She sounded totally insensitive. But I'm not Muriel. Okay? This is *Nina*! Nina, you dope, you!"

"Did you come over here to fight again?"

"Oh, hold on, hold on. I didn't start that whole thing. And it didn't come out of nowhere, either. Something was going on with you, remember? You were just a little, little bit mad and jealous, huh? Huh, Mitch? Huh, Mitch?"

"Slow down! Sure I got upset; I admit it. I got upset when I heard about that other guy."

"But that's crazy! Totally irrational." Now it seemed they were going to have the all-out fight they had avoided last week. Good. She was ripe for a fight. In all trust and faith she had told him about Bobby Sadler—not to make him jealous, not to build herself up, not to *boast*, for God's sake, but to share with him one of the painful memories of her growing-up years. And in return she'd gotten first a jealous outburst, then a week of silence and being ignored. And who had broken that silence? Not Mitch.

"I suppose it's rational to dig up the past!"

"Dig up—! You *asked* me."

"And you told me all right. Didn't skip a detail."

Now she was stung. "I hurt your tender feelings? Well, who—gives—a—!" She snapped her fingers in his face. "It happened five *years* ago."

"Yeah? Well, you talked like it was yesterday. God damn, you were smiling. You *enjoyed* that whole memory."

"I did *not*!"

"I say you did."

"And I say you were the one who got us started on all that. 'What was the worst year of your adolescence?' That's just what you said. Like a . . . a . . . a . . . sociology professor! Next you'll tell me it's okay for guys to screw around, but *girls* should be *virgins*."

"You're being ridiculous and emotional. You're not making sense. Let me tell you something! I didn't rub *your* nose in what happened with me and Muriel, and Shelley."

"Oh, Muriel and Shelley," she said.

He smiled calmly, infuriating her further. Imagine, calling her emotional!

"I could have described them if I wanted to," he went on. "I could tell you about Shelley's hair—long, red-gold color, really gorgeous. Or the way Muriel had of moving her butt around in this cute, sassy way. I didn't tell you. I didn't want to compare."

"How smug," she burst out. "You just did tell me. You just managed to tell me. Now tell me something else. Are you going to flip anytime I look at another guy? Is that what it is?"

"Yes, probably," he said. "Probably I will flip, I'll go crazy, I'll beat you up, okay? Does that satisfy you?"

"Don't you dare ever touch me," she said, gritting her teeth. "Don't you *dare* ever touch me, ever lay a hand on me. You wouldn't last one second with me if you ever got rough. I don't go for that, I hate that, I think it's sick and disgusting!"

"Oh, calm down, Nina," he said. "You're so easy to bait. Do you really think I'd hit you? You think I'm that sort of guy? Is that what you think? If that's what you think, you might as well check out right now."

"Well, thanks a lot. Thanks a whole big bunch," she said inadequately. She was close to tears. Why had she come here? Why had she brought the plant? A humble gesture. *Are you going to humble yourself?*

On the radio someone was singing in a husky voice; the words, pleading and emotional, slipped between them. "Last night, we had a misunderstandin' . . . This mornin', baby, I'm sufferin' . . ."

"We better talk," Mitch said. He rocked back on his heels. A judicious pose. *He* wasn't close to tears.

"Just tell me . . . do you want . . . does it even matter . . ." she stuttered. Then, explosively, "I don't think you care if we make up or not!"

"Would I say we should talk if I didn't care?"

"Well . . . well . . . what about it then? What about this whole week? Where were you?"

"Where were *you?*"

"I'm here now."

"Yeah." He picked up the green wine bottle, tipped it over his mouth. A few drops fell out. "I don't know. You got so mad at me. I couldn't deal with it."

"I couldn't deal with your jealousy."

"Well, it's—I guess being jealous isn't so good, but it's natural. I mean, you might have tried to understand, been more understanding and—"

"I guess you think it was all my fault." Her lips trembled. "Is that what you're saying? Well, I resent that." She slapped the table, her cheeks burned. Only don't let me cry, she thought, *please*. "I really resent that, Mitch."

"God, you're still angry, aren't you? You're really, really still pissed."

To her surprise, at that moment she did begin to cry, but when he came to her, she pushed him away. "No! Don't! Don't you dare feel sorry for me."

He sat down on the bed and watched her. "What the hell is going on, Nina?"

"I wish I knew," she choked. "I'm not getting much help from you, either." She wiped her face. Then for a couple of minutes they just looked at each other, while on the radio somebody kept singing about love.

"I want a drink of water," Nina muttered, feeling drained. She went into the kitchen and drank thirstily. She filled the glass again and watered the polka-dot plant. "Plant likes water. Plant's happy I'm watering it."

"Give me a drink," Mitch said.

"A drink?" Nina turned to look at him. "I'd like to dump this right on you," she said, and spilled the rest of the water over his head.

He looked utterly surprised. Nina couldn't hold back a whinny of manic laughter. His curls flattened out, his face dripped, and a large damp spot appeared on his T-shirt. "Oh, I *did* it," she said, trying vainly to check her laughter.

"Well, now—" Mitch stood, shaking his head like a dog. "That does it, that really does it. You're just asking for it." He smiled.

"Mitch—" She leaped back, stumbled over a pile of clothes, and then he had her.

"You're just asking for it," he repeated. He hugged her hard, the breath went out of her, but she couldn't stop laughing at how surprised he'd looked when she dumped the water on him.

"Mitch . . . no . . . Come on, it was just . . . just a joke . . ." She was still laughing as they fell down on the bed together.

Chapter Ten

"Did you bring your laundry?" Mitch picked up his duffel bag.

"Left it downstairs in the hall." Nina popped his painter's cap on her head.

"Do you have change for the machines?" He pulled the cap down over her eyes. "I'm all out."

She rattled her pockets. "My treat."

They went down the stairs arm in arm. Since they had made up their fight, they spent even more time together than before. They both noticed that they had grown closer, were nicer to each other and more careful of each other's feelings.

Just before Thanksgiving Nina had called home and spoken to her mother. "Ma? I'm really sorry, but I don't think I can come back for the holiday. I've got tons of work . . ." True enough—she was behind in her reading and had two papers overdue—but the real reason was that she and Mitch hadn't wanted to be separated.

"It won't be the same without you, Nina," her mother had said. "Just Nancy, the little boys, and Grandma. Our table is shrinking every year."

Nina had weakened. "Maybe I should come home, Ma. I could study at home, too."

"No, no," her mother said firmly. "If it would be distracting to you, I don't want you to do that. We'll see you over Christmas. Right now your school work is more important."

Half relieved, half ashamed, Nina had wanted to say, Ma, don't be so nice to me! Instead, guiltily, she had lingered on the phone, asking about everyone in the family. Her mother had finally ended the conversation. "This is going to cost a fortune. Write a letter next time, Nina."

"Hot. Full. Normal load." Mitch punched buttons.

"Did I tell you that Professor Lehman said he would teach me to play racquetball sometime?" Nina poured in the soap.

"Nickiepie said that?"

"Mmm." Nina regretted telling Kim Ogun's nickname for Nicholas Lehman.

"Why'd he say that?"

"He knows I've never played, and he thinks it's the greatest game—"

"It's okay."

"—and he said he really liked turning people on to things he loved."

"Did he say that, Nina?" Mitch laughed. *"Turn people on to things?"*

"I don't know if he put it that way exactly; maybe those are my words. Anyway, he was just being nice."

"When did all this happen?"

"Yesterday, when I was working."

"He was in the office? I thought he just left you his notes and you typed away like a good little office mouse."

"Sometimes he comes in to do some work."

"I thought it was a pretty small place. From the way you talk, it doesn't sound much bigger than a closet."

"It is small."

"And you're using the only desk. So where's Nickie-pie? Sitting in your lap?"

"He uses a student chair, writes on the armboard."

"Not very comfortable for a great man. Was he there all the time you were working?"

Nina stuffed a sheet into the washer before replying. "You make it zound zo zinister. Yezz, zee profezzor waz in zee offize wiz me, Inzpector Beerz." She wriggled her eyebrows. "All zee time I was typing zee zecret paperz for him."

"Yuk, yuk." He pulled the cap over her eyes again.

They sat down next to the window to wait for their laundry. Nina brought out knitting from a plastic bag. A new occupation: she had been seized with the desire to make something for Mitch. He yawned. "Tired?" she asked.

"Sleepy."

They looked at each other and smiled. A private smile. Nina held up the half-finished sock. "These are going to be really warm. I love this forest-green color, don't you?"

"Think you'll ever finish? You've been working on that one sock for weeks."

They sat knee to knee. The door opened. A bunch of students came in, and cold air with them. Yesterday Professor Lehman had asked Nina if she had a boyfriend. She had tried to explain about Mitch, why he'd dropped out of college. "One of those young men who think pounding nails is the better way?" he'd said.

Nina had defended Mitch's choice, but she had stumbled under Nicholas Lehman's ironical smile and was glad when he changed the subject to his daughter. Mindy's picture was tacked on the bulletin board: a small, sneakered girl, squinting into the sun, standing with her hands on a bicycle. She lived with her mother in Asheville, North Carolina.

Cradling a Styrofoam coffee cup, Nicholas Lehman spoke of how much he missed the child. "I get her for the summer. It's terrific when she's here, but I have to wait all year for that. I would have held the marriage together—for Mindy's sake. But her mother . . No, Claudia wasn't interested."

Nina listened, saying little, her eyes on his face. That he was talking to her in this way surprised and humbled her. She touched the thin silver hoops in her ears—a present from Mitch. She knew she had something of a schoolgirl crush on Nicholas Lehman. When she and Mitch first started going out together, it had bothered her that she still was ga-ga over the other man. But she'd worked out for herself that her feelings for Mitch were one thing; for her professor, entirely different and separate.

She loved Mitch and he loved her. Mitch was, well, *real*. Sometimes he smelled of machine oil or paint; he yawned and burped; he wore socks with holes in the toes, and left half-opened cans of food on the counter to rot. She didn't—couldn't—think of Nicholas Lehman in those terms.

He was like a movie star (in fact, he somewhat resembled an older Warren Beatty with a beard) ; he was like someone she might read about in *People* magazine, someone she could daydream about or put into her fantasies, but not someone you would expect to be part of your ordinary, everyday life.

And yet here he was talking to her, softly, intimately; leaning toward her as if it were important to him that she understand about his marriage. "It was a mistake. Sure, you can say hindsight—and you wouldn't be wrong." (Nina wouldn't have dared say any such thing. Wouldn't even have thought it. If the marriage had been wrong, surely it hadn't been his fault. Claudia—didn't that just conjure up an image of a cold, smiling blonde!) "But, Mindy," he went on, "Mindy came out of that. . . ."

There was appeal in his blue eyes. *Do you understand?* he seemed to be saying. *Do you see why I am the way I am? I smile, I joke, but the smile covers pain.*

Leaning toward him, Nina noticed a thin spot in the waves of his hair. Oh, poor man! she thought. And she wondered if his wearing the same, elbow-patched tweed jacket day in and day out was, after all, style, or the outward sign that he was neglected in the way that a man without a woman is neglected.

Afterward, when he was again sitting in the student chair by the window and she was again typing, Nina was intensely aware of him; her whole back was warm. She sat up straight at the typewriter, but made more mistakes than she ever did when she was alone.

But of all this she said nothing to Mitch, only mentioning the least important part, that Professor Lehman had made a casual remark about teaching her to play racquetball. She couldn't very well not ever talk about Nicholas Lehman—working for him, he was too much a part of her daily life—but she was careful what she said to Mitch. Why make him unhappy? His jealousy annoyed her, but it also made her want to laugh. Did he really think there were legions of men out there waiting to snatch her away from him!

She leaned toward him now and kissed him. "I'm hungry, I'm getting really hungry."

"After that big breakfast I fed you?" He brushed her hair off her face.

"It's the cold weather. I'm always hungry in cold weather."

"Let's get roast beef sandwiches when the laundry's done. My treat."

"You treated me last time."

"I just got paid yesterday, Nins. What am I going to do with all my money?"

"I'll pay my half. I'm working, too."

"I don't think you'll get rich in that job, sweetie. . . . Nina?" He nudged her foot with his. "I've been thinking—I want you to move in with me."

"Move in with you?"

He nodded. "I woke up this morning and I thought about it. And I realized it's ridiculous for you to live in one place and me in another. As it is you spend more time at my place than yours."

"Not really," she said.

"Yeah, really," he said. "You're already half moved in. You've got stuff all over. The other morning—did I tell you this?—I put your T-shirt on."

"You didn't." She laughed.

"I did, before I realized. . . ."

"Which one?"

"That blue one you left, the one that says I'D RATHER BE IN DENVER."

"I left that? I must have forgotten it last week."

Nearly everyone had left the campus for the long Thanksgiving weekend. Lynell had gone home with Sonia, and Nina found their empty apartment dim and depressing. After her first night alone she had packed up Emmett and spent the rest of the holiday with Mitch. The weather had turned sleety, and they had stayed in nearly the whole time.

"So, what do you think?" Mitch said.

"Move in," she repeated. Funny how her mind worked. Imagining the two of them living together, the first thing she thought about was food. He liked a big breakfast. She didn't. Then she thought about studying at the library table evenings while he read in the old velvet chair. She almost hummed at that image. And they'd go to bed together, wake up together. Their toothbrushes would nudge each other in the same jar in the bathroom.

She got up to put the wet wash into one of the drum dryers. Machines whirred and hummed on every side. A boy and girl folded clothes together at the long yellow folding table. Mitch came back from the candy machine with a chocolate bar that he broke in half for the two of them.

"You want us to live together," she said.

"It would make life a lot simpler for you," he said, standing close to her. "You'd be done with all this coming and going stuff."

"Yes . . ." She found herself a little disappointed that he sounded so practical. But what did she want? Him down on his knees? Nina, wilt thou move in with me? Had her father proposed to her mother on his knees? Even if he had (she knew he hadn't; family history had it that his head was under the hood of his car when he popped the question), it was utterly different. One was marriage, and one was living together. *L.T.* Then she thought of her parents again, and she knew that if she moved in with Mitch she could never tell them.

She pushed those thoughts away, went back to more practical considerations. Furniture. She didn't have much: a rug, a pair of curtains she'd never used, her cot, a few other things. Her room was so small at Sonia and Lynell's apartment. If she moved in with Mitch, she could really fix up his place—no, it would be *their* place. Nina's and Mitch's.

"You know what my father calls it when people live together?" she said.

"Don't tell me, I can guess."

"Shacking up."

"Well, look, it doesn't lessen my respect for your father, but that is a pretty narrow-minded point of view."

"I agree; you don't have to convince me."

"My father lived with his girl friend before they got married."

"Yes, but your father is a professor."

Mitch laughed. "Meaning?"

"Well, my parents . . . You know what a small town I come from—"

"Oh, I see. Professors are exotic types. Not like your average Mom and Pop mortals." Nina nodded. "Well, he's still just Pop to me," Mitch said. "And to tell the truth, I think the problem with him and his girl friend was that they didn't live together *long* enough. Five or six months, and they got married. And the next year, divorced. Now he's married again, but he and Cynthia lived together for four years first."

"They haven't been married very long, have they?"

"Not quite a year yet. Not long enough to know if it's going to last."

"After four years? That was like marriage, too, wasn't it?"

Mitch shrugged. "I'm just being realistic. Look at my parents. Seventeen years and then they divorced. You'd think people would stay together after seventeen years."

"My parents have been married thirty years." Nina opened the dryer to check the clothes, then snapped it shut and put in another quarter. "Do you want to get married someday, Mitch?"

"Someday, definitely."

"Me, too. I want kids, but not yet, not for a long time. Not till I'm twenty-eight or twenty-nine."

"Maybe they'll be my kids," Mitch said.

Nina squeezed his hand. "They could be as cute as you and—"

"I'm not *cute*, Nina."

"Yes, you are. I'm not the only one who thinks so. That's what Sonia said about you. I told you, didn't I? 'That Mitch is *cute*.' Mitch, listen. What if we decided to do this, and thirty years from now we're telling our kids about it? Telling them how one morning, in the Laundromat, we decided to live together. How we thought it would be for now, but it turned out to be forever."

"Sweetie, forever is an absurd word. Nobody knows what the future is going to bring."

"Well, I guess that's true."

"No guess about it. *I* don't know the future. *You* don't know the future. No one knows the future. Anyone who did could clean up. That person would have their *mil* a long time before old D.G. ever sees his. . . . So, Nina, what about it? Do you want to do it?"

She sat down again and took out her knitting, telling herself to be thoughtful rather than impulsive, but knowing that her mind was already made up. Wasn't everything in favor of the move? First and foremost, they were in love. Then, they were spending so much of their time together that it really would make life simpler, especially for her. Simpler and better. Much better. Irrelevantly, she wished she'd been the one to ask Mitch. Then she wondered where they'd keep Emmett's litter box, and after that she thought, Well, for once I'll have something that Lynell and Sonia don't have.

"I can't just walk out on Lynell and Sonia," she said, doing penance for her petty thought.

"I'm sure they can find another roommate," he said. "There are always people around looking to move."

"It can't be just anyone."

"Right. Somebody good will show up."

"And something else. It's not only me that moves in, Mitch. It's Emmett, too."

"Sure, it is. Love you, love your cat. Anything else?"

"Well . . . money."

"It won't cost you any more, Nina. I don't pay that much rent. We'll split everything down the middle, okay? Food shouldn't be any different."

"I should think about it some more," she said. "This is important. I shouldn't just rush into it."

"I agree," he said, "but it's not as if we just met. Nina . . . I want you to move in." His hand covered hers. "I really want you to do this."

"I really want to, too, Mitch . . . but it's a big step. We should think about it."

"I have. That's why I asked you."

"What if I'd asked you?" Nina said.

"I'd have loved it," he said. "Did you think about asking me?"

"No, I just wish I had. Why didn't I think of it first?"

He laughed. "We can pretend you did. Ask me, Nina. Ask me to live with you. See what I say."

"Mitch, what if we don't get along?"

"Why wouldn't we? We get along fine now."

"We fight. We fight a lot."

"And then we make up," he said.

"What happens if you hate living with me?"

"I won't. You could hate living with me, though."

She shook her head. "No, I won't. I've been thinking the dumbest things, Mitch. Our toothbrushes together . . ."

"Our shoes side by side . . . Nina, it will be so fine and great living together. Don't you think so?" he said anxiously.

She put her hands on his shoulders so that they were looking at each other full face. "Okay," she said after a moment.

"Okay?" A smile broke over his face.

She nodded. How extraordinary, how wonderful, to be able to make someone else so happy!

The Laundromat was packed by now. Standing by the steamy window, they put their arms around each other in a long, warm hug. *I'm going to remember this,* Nina thought. *I'll never forget this moment.*

Chapter
Eleven

On a cold, bright Saturday in December, Nina moved into Mitch's apartment. Sonia, Lynell, and D.G. all helped in the move. Not far to go, about three blocks, but as none of them had a car, everything had to be hand-carried. In short order Nina noticed that even a box of clothes that started out light in The Lion's Arms ended up heavy by the time it was lugged through Mitch's doorway.

Although she hadn't come to school with a lot of stuff, Nina had managed to accumulate enough to keep them busy for a couple of hours. "If I'd known it would be this much work, I wouldn't have been so quick to move," she said.

"Too late for regrets," Lynell said. "You're stuck, baby."

Nina had been pleasantly surprised when Lynell and Sonia volunteered to help. When she'd first told them she was planning to move in with Mitch, they had not been happy. "That is a hell of a note," Sonia said. "You realize you're going to leave us in the lurch?"

"I'm not making the move until you find someone else," Nina protested. "You don't think I'd do that, do you?"

"And what if we don't find someone else? It's pretty late in the season, you know. People have made their arrangements a long time ago."

Nina's heart sank. "We'll find someone else. I'm sure we will."

She had been right. Later that same day Helen Wander, another music student, would move into Nina's vacated room. Helen, also a singer, had had a serious fight with her boyfriend a few days after Nina had made her announcement. When Sonia mentioned that Nina was moving out and that she and Lynell were looking for another roommate, Helen took it as a sign from heaven that she was meant to leave her boyfriend.

The whole time they were moving Emmett was underfoot, rushing to the door every time it opened. There were constant cries of, "No, Emmett! . . . Out of the way, Emmett . . . Emmett, get *back*." Finally, when only dustballs were left in her room, Nina carried the cat downstairs. At the smell of fresh air his nose turned bright pink and twitched wildly.

"You should have a leash for him," Mitch remarked. "He's as big as a dog."

"Wait till you see the way she feeds him," Lynell said. "Now that you're leaving, Nina, I can tell you that I've never liked your dear Emmett that much."

"I always knew that," Nina said calmly, as if Lynell's remark didn't hurt.

In Mitch's place, Nina showed Emmett his box in the bathroom and his food dish in the kitchen. She left him to sniff around the jumble of boxes while they all went out to eat.

"Here's where it all began," Mitch said when they walked into the sandwich shop. "Let's take the same table." He and Nina sat close together. She liked the way he looked in a dark blue sweatshirt and sneakers.

"I thought you met on a ladder," Sonia said.

"Yeah, true; Nina was giving me the eye all the time I was painting. Then she followed me in here, and after that, she wouldn't leave me alone."

"Sonia and I met in the park last year," D.G. said. "She caught my Frisbee. Come on, now, folks, don't laugh. That's literally true."

Nina was tremendously excited. She couldn't stop laughing and smiling. I want to remember this, she told herself again. Mitch . . . my friends. . . . They were all smiling benignly at her. They had ordered a huge amount of food. Pizza, sandwiches, cookies, and frosted cakes. Mitch's treat. There was good will in the air. Sonia caressed D.G.'s neck, and Lynell said almost wistfully, "Too bad Adam couldn't make it." As if Nina's moving in with Mitch was a special occasion to be shared with those closest to you.

All at once the old childhood rhyme flashed into Nina's mind. *Nina and Mitch sitting in a tree, k-i-s-s-i-*

n-g! First comes love, then comes marriage, then comes Nina with a BABY carriage! She moved closer to Mitch, pressing her leg against his. Of course she wasn't thinking of marriage, neither of them was, but all the same . . .

"Well, now, Mitch," Lynell said, glancing obliquely at him through her hair, "you have someone to do the cooking and cleaning, right?"

"It's not going to be like that," Nina said. "We're going to share everything."

"Ninny, I was baiting Mitch, not you."

"You need better bait for me." Lazily Mitch curled his hand through Nina's hair.

"I'll remember that. I happen to be a very good fisherman." Lynell and Mitch had established a kind of teasing rapport. It had happened only this morning. Over Emmett, Nina thought. Mitch wasn't an enthusiastic cat lover, either, and the two of them had batted Emmett jokes back and forth. "Let's enroll him in a diet workshop." "Oh, I don't know, why don't we just admit his useful years are past and make a cat scarf out of him?" and when Nina protested that none of that was very humorous, they had only laughed harder at the spectacle of her so passionately defending her beloved cat. She consoled herself with the thought that living with Emmett, Mitch would learn to love him as she did. She certainly wasn't going to let herself get too upset over what had to be a minor flaw in Mitch's character. Her cheeks were steaming, and she burst out suddenly, "Do any of you guys think of yourself as an animal?"

"Sure," Sonia said immediately. "I'm a cat." She purred.

"And I'm Bozo, the faithful dog," D.G. said, lolling his head on Sonia's shoulder.

Nina added to the merriment by saying that she was a donkey. For years she'd had that mental image of herself, head down, pushing along stubbornly. And who, she had thought, would ever love a donkey? She had become that donkey that moment in Mr. Pretorious's office. After, secretly terrified, she had forced herself to keep her promise . . . or vow . . . or resolution—whatever it was. She was going to college. She had plugged along, going her donkey way, her mostly solitary way. She had said it; now she had to make it happen. And all the time yearning for other things: for love, for friendship, for touching and closeness. For someone else, for the *other,* that *someone* who would say, *Let's spend the day together. . . . Let's . . . Let us* . . . Us is what she had yearned for. Nina and . . . *someone.*

She had had crushes on this one and that one, on boys in her classes, teachers, and men she passed for a moment in the street. But everything had happened only in her head. She looked, thought, yearned, wished, wanted. Silently. All in secret. And said to herself, Someday . . . someday . . . Someday my prince will come? But she didn't believe in princes. Or maybe what she didn't believe was that *she* was a princess whom a prince would seek out.

She was plain Nina Bloom. And yet, here was Mitch. Who had walked into her life. Who had seen her from a ladder. Who had liked what he saw. And still liked her. Loved her. And she loved him. It *was* a miracle. Mitch. . . . This tall, soft-eyed boy-man. Couldn't he have had any girl? Shouldn't he have wanted some other girl? Wanted a Sonia, flushed and pretty, dimpled, with silver wound around her wrists? Or a Lynell, tall and slender, sophisticated, her beautiful hair falling down her back? But he wanted *her*. Try to tell her that wasn't a miracle!

They sat in the shop for a long time. "I'm *stuffed*," D.G. declared. Paper cups, crumpled napkins, and bits of cakes littered the table. When they got up to leave, Nina embraced Sonia and then Lynell. "We'll be seeing plenty of you, for God's sake," Lynell said, but hugged her back.

"You have to invite us over for supper or something," Sonia said.

"Don't forget me," D.G. said.

"Oh, D.G., I couldn't forget you. Thank you, everyone. Thank you, all of you." Nina's eyes were wet. And walking away with Mitch, walking down the street hand in hand, she thought again that she was now part of the "us" she had so much longed for. No more just Nina. Now it was Nina and Mitch.

In the morning, waking, Nina saw boxes, the legs of a table, and a laundry bag lying collapsed on top of a rolled-up rug. She had been dreaming about feet. . . . A tall woman, a Paul Bunyan of a woman, and enormous feet. How odd. *Your feet, your big feet,* someone had said in her ear.

Next to her Mitch slept with the sheet wrapped

around his neck. He looked almost angelic, his lower lip softly drooping. But with his eyes closed, his soul was closed to her; and suddenly he seemed to Nina, in the most profound way, unknown, unknowable. A stitch of panic ran through her. Who was he, really? She had moved in with a stranger. *Why?*

She couldn't assemble her reasons. Her feelings had fled. In the half-light of morning, filtered through the disorder in the room, everything came to her with a pang, a distant, dreamlike beat. She remembered making love, the lovemaking itself like a dream in which she saw ships, white sails, blue waves. She had been exhausted, half asleep.

"Hello," Mitch said, opening his eyes. "Hello, Nina, what a nice surprise." He moved his foot against hers.

"Hello," she said tentatively.

"Did you sleep okay?"

"Yes, fine."

"What's that crazy cat doing?" Mitch raised himself on an elbow, just as Emmett buried his head under a clump of newspapers.

"He's playing ostrich," Nina said. "One of his morning games." With each word the strangeness receded. She touched Mitch's hand. "Hi," she said with relief.

Just then the phone rang. "Wonder who that is." Mitch stretched, pulling the phone closer to the bed.

"Wait," Nina said. "Don't answer. What if it's my mother?"

"Your mother?" He laughed at her. "She doesn't know you're here, does she?"

"No, that's the point," Nina said, holding his arm. "I don't want her to know! She can't know, Mitch."

"Honey, if she doesn't know, how could she be calling?" Mitch said reasonably. The phone rang again, and he picked it up. "Oh, hi, Kenny." He winked reassuringly at Nina.

Out on the street she heard the whine of a motorcycle. Inside, Emmett, hungry, pounced on dustballs. Of course it couldn't be her mother. She didn't know Mitch's phone number. She hardly knew he existed. Nina had walked into this life without her mother's knowledge, had walked in on her own two big feet.

She fell back against the pillow. So that was what the dream had been telling her. Was it also reminding her that whatever she did, wherever and however far her feet took her, they could never take her far enough to forget that her mother was her mother, and that somehow, in some way, she, Nina, had finally to answer to her . . . as well as to herself?

Chapter Twelve

Living with Mitch was certainly different from living with Sonia and Lynell. Not in just the obvious ways: that it was *he* and *she,* that they were male and female, slept in the same bed and were lovers. What took Nina by surprise was the extraordinary degree of intimacy. It wasn't just living in a single room, though that, of course, was part of it. But what she hadn't expected was that although each of them had a routine, almost at once they began to mesh, to do as much as possible at the same time.

Stayed up late together because Nina was hyper, or crawled into bed early because Mitch was wiped out. Mornings, Mitch nearly always woke up first, but they turned out of bed at the same time. After a struggle over breakfast, they began to take most of their meals together. Nina passed up a movie she wanted to see because it would have meant going alone: Mitch knew he'd be bored by it. On the other hand she did get to a Sandy Big Tree Band concert that, alone, she definitely would have overlooked.

They liked being together. Naturally! That was why they were living together. *Like* was really too pale a word. They craved being together. They crowded into the kitchen together to cook, they showered together, they cleaned and shopped together, and for weeks hardly saw anyone else.

Something was going on: a melding of their individuality, the habits that were unique to each of them. Nina had wanted it, wanted that us-ness. Still, it came as something of a revelation to her. The process began almost immediately after she moved in.

"What is this?" Mitch said as Nina wandered around the room holding a cup. It was a weekday morning.

"What is what?" she said fuzzily. She was never fully awake first thing in the morning.

"Don't you sit down for breakfast? I mean, a real breakfast, not a cup of coffee."

"Sure. Saturday . . . Sunday. Oh, good, here it is." She found the shirt she wanted, still packed in a box of clothes.

"I've noticed the way you eat. It's a little nutty, Nins. Breakfast on the fly, and not much of it. Not a real good way to start the day."

"I know, you're right. I've read all those articles about having a big breakfast, too. . . ." She put down the cup, yawning, and buttoned her shirt. "But I don't have time on school mornings." The radio was on. The moment Mitch rolled out of bed, he turned it on. Loud. Nina winced as the announcer blared out the weather forecast for at least the fifth time. "Rainy and *cold* this morning, so *bundle up* and take your *umbrellas,* good buddies—"

"Do you have to have that on so loud?"

"What?" His turn to be bewildered.

"The radio. That idiot voice!"

"I hardly hear him." He turned the volume down.

"Do you even listen?" Nina fumbled in the drawer for a pair of tights. Damn. The toes were totally gone on her favorite green pair.

"I hear enough. I pick up the news this way." He took her by the elbow and steered her to the table. "Sit, honey."

"Mitch, I don't have my pants on."

"Oops, sorry. Get them on. Then sit."

"Gosh, I feel like a dog," she complained as she pulled on tights and jeans.

Mitch had put out rolls, jelly, a box of cereal, milk and eggs.

"Boiled eggs? Vile!"

"Next time I'll scramble them." He sat down next to her, tapping an egg with a knife.

"Don't bother. I can't face eggs in the morning. Not even for you."

"Eggs are the food of life. Full of protein. That coffee is empty calories."

She leaned on her hand, looking at him sideways. "You should have warned me you were a reformer before I moved in."

"I'm sneaky." He poured Rice Chex into a dish and pushed it in front of her. "My family always sat down together for breakfast."

"Not mine." Nina poured milk onto the Rice Chex, and dutifully chewed a spoonful. "There were so many of us, all going in different directions." Odd how hard it was to fight the feeling that Mitch's family was, well, not superior to hers, but somehow a family that knew how to do things better or more correctly.

Mitch didn't let up on his campaign for Nina to eat breakfast, and she began getting up earlier to have time for the food he made. One morning it would be pizza (on an English muffin), the next morning pancakes or French toast drowned in syrup. She didn't find it easy to face so much food that early in the morning. While they ate, she forbade herself to look at the clock, but as soon as they were done, the scramble was on. Sometimes they stacked the dirty dishes into the sink, more often left everything on the table. "Later . . . I'll clean up later." Since Mitch cooked, it was only fair that she do the clean-up. Feeling overfull, she gathered books and notebooks, pulled on a jacket, and rushed out. Halfway down the stairs—this happened to her half a dozen times—she rushed back, suddenly anxious that Mitch, still not tuned to Emmett's ways, might have accidentally let him out.

"You worry about the cat like he's a kid," Mitch said one night.

"Well, in a way, he is my baby. It would kill me if anything happened to him."

"Nothing's going to happen to him, Nins. Cats are smart; they're instinctive."

"Ha. I heard you calling him dumbbell this morning."

Mitch snickered. "Well, on the cat scale of intelligence . . . Admit it, he doesn't rate genius."

Nina kissed Emmett on his broad face. "Don't listen to him, darling."

"I don't see how you can do that. Doesn't it bother you that he cleans himself with his tongue? I mean that tongue goes everywhere."

"Here, why don't you try kissing him?"

"No, thanks."

"Come on, Mitch, kiss him." Holding Emmett out, Nina advanced on Mitch. "Kiss him, Mitch. Don't be in a rut. Don't be so narrow-minded." Two of Mitch's favorite words.

"Think you're funny, don't you?"

"Yeah!" She followed him around the room. "Kissy, kissy, Mitchy! Come on, make friends with Emmett. You two boys have to get along."

"Nina, you big bully, take that cat away from my face."

Emmett settled the matter by jumping out of Nina's arms and stalking away, his ears perked indignantly.

For days on end the weather was frigid and gray. Nina rushed home from work, usually arriving before Mitch. Dump books, kick off shoes, turn on radio (he liked music in the background all the time), start supper. While the water boiled for spaghetti she'd run hot, soapy water into the sink for the breakfast dishes.

Next, she'd storm through their room, straightening
the bed, setting the table, and pushing clothes into
the closet and the bureau. Then Mitch would come.
"Hello!" He'd smile, drop his lunch pail, kiss her with
breath that smelled metallic and sour. He'd go into
the bathroom to shower, change his clothes, brush his
teeth, and she'd sit on the edge of the tub talking to
him about her day. By the time he was in fresh clothes
and had shaved, he was getting his second wind and
she was running down as fast as a clock that needed
rewinding. But food and wine or beer restored her.
She ate and drank hungrily, her turn now to listen to
his tales.

They were snug in their room. If the heat went off,
they got into bed. Nothing bothered them. If they ran
out of bread or Band-Aids or bath powder, they bun-
dled up and went out together to shop. On the street
they walked with their arms around each other in a
tight embrace, and later, back in their room, while
Nina studied, Mitch would sit near her, reading and
stroking her hair. Lovely . . . oh, lovely. . . Like a cat
herself, Nina moved closer to Mitch.

Chapter Thirteen

"So! How are you guys doing?" Sonia said one day, meeting Nina on the street just as she came out of the cheese store across from her old apartment.

"Great!" Nina said. "Why don't you and Lynell come over and visit us?"

"I wouldn't want to spoil the honeymoon."

"Oh . . . the honeymoon!" Nina rolled her eyes. "God, we haven't seen anyone in ages. We're total hermits."

"Still love each other?"

Nina smiled.

"So it was a good move?" Sonia said.

"Did you doubt?"

"You never know about these things. . . ."

"I guess not." But she hadn't had doubts. That was

the good part of being impulsive. When things worked out, you could say, airily, *Oh, I always knew it was going to be okay.* . . . "How are you doing, Sonia? How's D.G.?"

"No complaints. He was asking about you the other day."

"He was, really? I like D.G.; he's a sweet guy."

"He has his good points," Sonia said.

"Listen," Nina said impulsively, warmed by the contact, "I want you all to come over." She took Sonia's arm. "You and Lynell and D.G. and Adam. Come over for breakfast on Sunday." It would be nice to have company. A change of pace, something different to look forward to—and she wouldn't mind, at all, showing off a bit: how they lived, how they'd fixed up the place, how close they were. "We'll have a big, gorgeous gorge. Mitch's specialty is breakfast."

The next morning, combing her hair, she remembered the meeting with Sonia and mentioned the invitation. "Sonia's going to pass it on to everyone else, okay?"

"Too late not to be okay."

She leaned into the mirror. "Hey, you don't mind, do you?" She was pleased with the way she looked . . . something about her face. . . . Maybe her expression? Or was it her eyes? Were they bigger? Silly. But, really, she did look good. "Sweetie? Do you mind? I thought you'd like it."

"Sure, but—"

"What?"

"Well, what if I'd planned on doing something else?"

"We didn't talk about anything else. Was there something else you had in mind?"

"I've been thinking it might be fun to go tobogganing."

"It would be! But we can do that another weekend, okay?"

"Okay, okay."

"Grump, grump. You just want to make all the decisions."

"Hey, this is a democracy."

"Oh, sure." But she'd noticed that he *did* like to be in charge; to say yes, no, maybe, right, wrong . . . just like her father, her brothers. . . . Oh, well . . . She hugged him. "It'll be fun. You can cook your Hawaiian rice." An incredible concoction he'd introduced her to that put fried eggs, bananas, and rice on the same breakfast plate.

For the rest of the week, in odd moments, Nina would imagine the coming Sunday get-together: the things the other four would say, how they'd look at her and Mitch, how impressed they'd be. She imagined Sonia whispering to Lynell, *I don't know anyone else as close as Mitch and Nina. . . .*

How pleasant it would be to talk openly about the two of them! She had to censor the letter she wrote home. After news about herself (classes, marks, her job for Professor Lehman), she would pop in a casual mention of Mitch. "My boyfriend . . ." And that was it. Undoubtedly enough. They were probably jumping for joy because she finally *had* a boyfriend. She'd once heard her mother saying to her father, "They're all over Nancy like flies, but Nina . . ." And then,

"But she's got brains. She's going to make something of herself." When her mother wrote to Nina, it would always be on a sheet of lined paper with, first, news about the other kids, and then reminders to study hard and get enough sleep. The last thing her mother would imagine was that not only did Nina have a lover, but that she was living with him.

No, being open with her family was impossible. Yet she wanted to talk about herself and Mitch. Chafing, she looked for others to tell. Sitting next to freckled Kim Ogun in Nicholas Lehman's lit class, whenever possible Nina dropped Mitch's name into the conversation. "Mitch and I went for a walk. . . . You'll never believe what Mitch made for supper. . . . Oh, Mitch and I saw that TV show, too." But, somehow, sharp Kim never caught on, or, anyway, never asked the pointed questions that would lead to Nina's saying (she had rehearsed it), *We talked it over, and I moved in with him. Right. I'm living with my boyfriend, and it's working out. It's really great.*

Oddly, though, without meaning to, she blurted the whole thing out to Professor Lehman one afternoon. The weather was dismal; freezing rain ran down the small window, and inside the tiny office, the old rusty pipes running across the ceiling clanked ceaselessly. Around four o'clock Nicholas Lehman called for a coffee break and offered Nina a sticky roll from a paper bag he took out of his briefcase.

"Thanks," she said, taking one. "It looks just like what I had for breakfast. My boyfriend bought them. He's always trying to get me to eat more at breakfast." Then she heard herself, and she saw from the expression on Nicholas Lehman's face that he understood perfectly. Putting down the roll, she stared hard at the paper she'd just typed. Blabbermouth! Of all people to tell! Kim Ogun was one thing, but Professor Lehman . . . No, no, *no*. Now what would he think of her? She didn't think less of herself for moving in with Mitch, but Professor Lehman was another generation. He wasn't *old*, but he wasn't her age, either.

"My wife and I lived together for a while before we got married," he said in a moment, in an easy tone.

She looked up and blurted, "We're not thinking of getting *married*!" Damn. Damn, damn, damn. Foot in the mouth again. In case he hadn't been completely sure of the situation . . . Living together—and not even because they were engaged and planning marriage.

"I should hope not," he said. "You're far too young for marriage."

"Well . . ." She smiled weakly. How tactful he was! How nice! How very, very nice.

"How old are you, Nina?" he asked. When she first began working, it had been Miss Bloom, everything very correct. But back then she would never have imagined their having this conversation.

"Almost twenty."

"Ahh," he said, but now he didn't even seem to be talking to her anymore. He'd turned and was looking out the window, with an expression on his face that sent a pang through Nina. Oh, she could guess what he was thinking. Feeling sorry that he wasn't twenty or twenty-one anymore. She wished she had the nerve to tell him that he was a lot more interesting and attractive than most guys half his age. Excluding Mitch, of course!

Was it awful of her to feel sorry for him? But he had had a sad life. His wife had left him, and he missed his little daughter like anything. He was always showing Nina Mindy's drawings and letters. He had the latest one tacked up on the bulletin board. "Dear Dady, I hat being clean, but Momy insits ever day Mindy get your hair combed. Mindy get your hair comb! Its not a free world dear Dady no its not a free world. Not free for me. When its comes to parents sometimes I get sick!!! Well so long for now dear Dady, love, Mindy Lehman."

Sitting still at the typewriter, Nina imagined herself rising, walking to Nicholas Lehman, stroking his hair . . . imagined him turning to her with a grateful smile, taking her hand, holding it to his cheek . . . Or, no, she'd just go to him, say, "Don't be sad . . . I'm sure you'll find someone else to love. . . ."

"I could use a good type eraser," she said briskly, scrabbling in the Dundee Marmalade jar that held his pens and pencils. "Or some of that instant erase tape."

"Why don't you pick it up, Nina? I'll reimburse you." He raised the venetian blind, then lowered it halfway. Silly to have anything on that window. All they could see out was feet and the bottoms of legs. Every once in a while someone's face would appear, a curious student bending down, looking in. A wave, a grin, and they'd be off.

Nicholas Lehman stirred, crumpled the paper bag, and threw it across the room into the wastebasket.

"Hey, yay!" Nina clapped.

His blue eyes gleamed, his face brightened. He crumpled a piece of paper, took aim, threw. The paper fell neatly into the basket. "Want to see me do that again?" His face was rosy, like a boy's.

"Sure. Anytime."

"Can I be on your team?"

"Sure. Anytime."

They were flirting. She was flirting; so was he. Her face was warm; she couldn't stop smiling. The way he was looking at her . . . and his eyes were so *blue*. They were like blue lights. He lit his pipe, looking at her over the stem. When she began typing again, her hands were moist.

Chapter Fourteen

Sunday morning Nina and Mitch planned to get up early in order to clean up some of the accumulated debris in their place before their guests arrived. But the room was cold—they could see their breath puffing into the air—and they huddled down into the blankets. "I bet that cheap landlord has got the heat off again," Mitch said. In the hall they heard someone yelling about complaining to the mayor's office. "Go to it," Mitch yelled between cupped hands.

Nina rubbed her nose against his shoulder. "Do you think we bought enough rolls? Darn! I just remembered—we're out of jam."

"Let them eat butter. Stop worrying, Nins."

"Well . . . our first company. It's important. I'm excited. Aren't you excited, Mitch?"

"Yeah, sure I am," he admitted.

"Should we wash the tub?"

"What for? We invited them to brunch, not to take a bath."

"Funny. But we've got ring around the tub."

"Pull the shower curtain. Better clean the catbox, though. You can smell that."

"I know, and the garbage should go out. Talk about smells!"

"Catbox, you. Garbage, me."

"Deal. Should we get up, then?"

"Nice day to stay in bed. Too bad they're coming. . . ."

"You don't *really* mind?" Nina sat up anxiously.

"Listen, as long as they eat my Hawaiian rice . . ."

She sprawled over him to look at the clock. "Oh, gosh, we don't have that much time left. We really better roll out, Mitch."

"Let's fool around a little first."

Nina shook her head, trying to look stern.

"Just a little?" he coaxed.

When they finally got up they barely had time to make the bed and get the food started before everybody arrived.

"It's like the North Pole in here." Lynell had her flute case under her arm. "I was going to serenade you two, but I don't think so. My fingers might fall off."

"The landlord doesn't believe in spoiling us with heat," Mitch said. "Hello, Lynell. Welcome to our humble abode. Do you drag that flute everywhere?"

"Oh, me and my flute are inseparable. Did you ever think, people, how much superior a flute is to a man?

Flute never gives orders, lies in its little velvet bed waiting for you . . . And when you say, 'Make music, flute,' you just blow a little, and presto, music."

Mitch laughed and hugged her. That set the tone. Nina hugged D.G., Adam kissed Sonia, and then they all switched around.

"Who'd I miss?" Sonia said. She took Mitch's head between her hands and kissed him on the mouth. "You look great. Living with Nina must be good for you."

"Nina, this place literally smells fantastic. What are you cooking?" D.G. sat down in the brown velvet chair and pulled Sonia onto his lap. "Guys, this place is cozy," he said. "Very, very cozy."

"Well, we've hardly fixed it up," Nina began modestly, but no one would hear a word of it. They insisted the place looked marvelous. Nina had covered the windowsills with plants, and she and Mitch had both tacked up pictures of their families on the wall. They also now had an official "couch"—Nina's old cot, covered with a blanket.

"How's your new roommate?" Mitch asked.

"Helen's okay," Lynell said. "No trouble, except when she and Sonia want to practice at the same time." Lynell and Sonia looked at each other and laughed. "Nina," Lynell went on, "Emmett looks fatter than ever. Is it possible?"

Sonia scooped up Emmett. "Missed you, baby. Next to my Heidi, I love you most. Adam, ever see such a big cat? How much does he weigh, Nina?"

"I don't know exactly. Sixteen or seventeen pounds, I think."

"Is there a Weight Watchers for cats?" Lynell asked, looking at Mitch.

Adam stroked Emmett with long fingers. "A beautiful cat, Nina." Adam, befitting his princely appearance, was wearing a gray silk vest. "I like him."

"Eh, he's such a beggar," Mitch said. "Every time Nina gives him food he purrs like a machine. And she thinks that he loves her for herself."

"He does," Nina said.

"It's not wrong that he loves her for feeding him," Adam said. "I'm sure he loves Nina for other things, too."

Well, that was nice. Nina wondered why her opinion of Adam had been so negative. Really, she hardly knew the guy. Unfairly—she saw now—she had concluded that he was irresponsible and low-down because he was caught in a sticky situation between Lynell and the Michigan girl friend. Why hadn't she realized that maybe he was just a sensitive person who dreaded hurting either Lynell or the other girl, and had got himself into this tight spot without meaning any harm?

"Lynell, you really don't like this cat?" he said. He looked at her, sort of pleadingly, Nina thought. She wished Lynell would look back with more warmth, but in a moment realized the two of them were having a fight. Oh! Now she understood the bit about the flute being better than a man. That had been meant for Adam. Too bad that they were fighting. It was much nicer the way Sonia and D.G. were hanging on each other. Maybe seeing them, plus how happy she and Mitch were, would inspire Adam and Lynell to make up.

"Look what we've got." Mitch brought out a bottle of pink champagne.

"I'll get swacked if I drink before I eat," Sonia said.

"Go ahead! Get swacked," D.G. said. "You're funny when you get swacked."

"Let's toast Nina and Mitch."

They clinked glasses. Adam made the toast, something about a "fine young couple," that was either half sardonic or totally sincere. Sincere, Nina decided, smiling at him and finishing her champagne. It was a little sharp, but warmed her from the stomach outward in one lovely glow.

"More, please." She held out her glass.

"Nina, you can't get swacked, you have to cook."

"Not me. Mitch is chief cook around here."

"Cookie, I'm getting hungry. Where's the chow?"

"One more glass of champagne . . ."

When the food was ready, Nina and Mitch brought everything out on a big tray. "Let's eat it while it's hot," Mitch said.

"*What* is it?" Lynell said.

"An adventure in eating," Nina said. "Hawaiian rice. You gotta be brave."

The room seemed to have become even colder. "My ears are warm," D.G. said, "but my feet are freezing, people."

"The only warm place is in bed," Mitch said ruefully.

"Breakfast in bed?" Sonia said. "Super idea."

In a minute it was arranged. They put the tray in the center of the bed, then arranged themselves around it, tucking blankets over their legs and feet. Sonia wound her pink scarf around her neck. Nina finished her champagne and put on an old green fur-lined hat her grandmother had bought at a thrift shop years ago. It had fur earlaps and strings that tied under her chin.

"That is an incredible hat," Lynell said, staring.

"Nina looks like Radar in M*A*S*H," Sonia said.

"Cute." Adam gave her a warm smile.

"All you need are the glasses, Nina, and you could try out for the show." Sonia was sitting between D.G. and Adam. "Come closer, you two, keep me warm. Oh, heavens, this is better than bundling."

"I'll drink to that," Mitch said.

Sonia clapped her hands. "I'm happy. I'm definitely happy right now."

"Oh . . . right now," Lynell said. She picked up her flute and blew a few notes. "That's the easy part. How about later? How about tomorrow?"

" 'Tomorrow and tomorrow and tomorrow,' " Sonia said grandly, holding out her glass for a refill. "Who knows about tomorrow? Who cares?"

"Anyway, what is happiness?" Mitch said.

"You and me!" Nina put her arm around Mitch. They all wriggled and snuggled closer. They held their plates on their laps and ate fast. The Hawaiian rice disappeared, and the basket of rolls, and a bowl of frosted cookies.

"This is a wonderful party, Nina and Mitchell,"

D.G. said. "I feel huppy, too. Happy," he corrected himself. "I'm getting stoned, people. I didn't think anyone literally got stoned on pink champagne."

"D.G.," Sonia said, "do you think you could not say literally for about half an hour and make *me* huppy?"

"Can try." D.G. covered his head with his arms and winked at Nina.

The whole idea of the six of them on the same bed—half *in* bed—struck Nina as incredibly sophisticated. Of course, nothing out of the way was going to happen, but all the same, it was a lot more interesting than if they'd been sitting around a table. Something had changed the moment they got on the bed. Some invisible barrier had gone down, and the amount of wine and champagne they were consuming didn't hurt, either. They were all talking in loud voices, interrupting each other, laughing at everything, and making as many jokes as possible.

"Adam, your feet are delicious and *toasty*," Sonia said. "D.G., darling, why do you have such damp feet all the time? I would like you to have hot, toasty feet."

"Cold feet, hot blood. Right, Lynell?" He squeezed the tall girl.

"Right, Donald George."

Sonia giggled. "Oh, oh, oh! You said it! You said it, Lynell. You said his name."

"Donald George, you don't like your name?" Lynell said innocently.

"I refuse to answer. I will literally ignore that comment. I repeat, Cold feet, hot blood."

"Old Croatian saying," Mitch said. "Man with cold feet has hot blood. Woman with cold feet better watch out."

"Oh, men!" That was Sonia. They were all laughing. It was silly time. Bashfully Nina made a joke, too. "You mean, Sonia, *ah,* men?" To her delight, that also got a laugh.

"That's my girl." Mitch held her hand up like a winning fighter.

Lynell took Nina's other hand. "Stick with us womens, little Nina, and you'll get further." Meant for Adam, of course. Of the three couples, only he and Lynell weren't sitting next to each other.

"She might get further," Mitch said, "but she won't have as much fun."

"Touché." Lynell reached across Nina and fed Mitch the last piece of her strawberry shortcake. He pretended to bite her fingers.

"Touché—isn't that what you Jewish people call your behinds?" D.G. said to Sonia.

"D.G.!" Sonia bumped him with her shoulder. "How come you've known me so long and you're still so ignorant? Tushy, D.G., *tushy,* as in my best friend in high school saying, 'Sonia, you have got a fat tushy.' "

"This conversation is literally getting out of hand."

"Oh, literally, my arse," Mitch said.

"No, literally your touché," Lynell said.

Mitch laughed, and reached across Nina to rub Lynell's head. "Hasn't this happened before?" Nina said.

"You're cute," Mitch said. Nina thought he meant her.

"No one has ever called me cute," Lynell said. "I don't think *cute* is my style."

"You are cute," Mitch insisted, talking across Nina.

She leaned back. "Go on, you two, enjoy yourselves. Don't let me get in your way."

"Oh, oh, Mitch, watch yourself, somebody is getting mad at somebody else," D.G. said.

"Nina's not mad at me. Nina never gets mad at me." He kissed her lightly, then with more pressure. They put their arms around each other and kissed. The others watching them, laughing and applauding, somehow made the kiss even more exciting. A warm current seemed to pass through them all. D.G. leaned toward Lynell. Sonia put her arms around Adam.

And Nina, sitting next to Mitch, her lips still warm from his mouth, found herself thinking about the other two guys. . . . Just looking at them and wondering . . . All three guys were so different. Mitch, nearly as tall as Adam, but sort of soft and sweet looking, despite being skinny. He had a little ring of fat around his waist. His baby fat, Nina teased. Adam was fatless, all long bones. And D.G. was chunky, muscular, more like a short football player than a Wall Street millionaire-to-be.

Nina smiled. Her mind was free and floating. Adam winked at her. She winked back. *Wink . . . wink . . .* Every man is a lover, she thought wisely. "D.G.—" She winked at him. *Wink . . . wink . . .* Mitch's turn. No playing favorites. *Wink . . . wink . . .* She giggled. "Guys, I'm swacked," she said, and suddenly flopped over, half asleep, into Mitch's lap.

Chapter Fifteen

Nina went home for Christmas. Had to. Either that or come clean with her family. Tell all. *Sorry, folks, can't make it home because I don't want to leave Mitch. He's got kinda used to me being around. . . .* Which, in fact, was one of the things he'd said when they were talking over the pros and cons of Nina's going home over the holidays. "I'm going to hate being alone."

"How about me?" she said.

"No, you'll be with your family. It won't be so bad for you." Mitch's family was scattered all over. His father had been teaching in Hawaii the past year, his mother, stepfather, and brother, Robert, were on vacation in England, and his sister, Trissy, was out in Oregon at Reed College.

"I'll miss you, though," Nina said.

"I'll miss you more. I'll have more time to miss you."

Again Nina considered coming up with some reason why she couldn't make it back home for Christmas. But she wanted to go home, wanted to see everyone. To be truthful, she hadn't missed them that much— most days passed without her thinking of her family at all—still, something was pulling her home.

"You know, I didn't go for Thanksgiving." Did she have to sound so apologetic? "They expect me," she added more briskly.

"Oh, I know," Mitch said glumly.

"You could come with me."

"Can I sleep in your bed?"

"Fat chance. You couldn't even sneak in. Nancy and I sleep in the same room."

"Yeah, yeah; you told me that."

"Okay, *sorry*." Were they going to fight now? Did he have to look so downcast? "It's only for a week."

"Closer to two weeks."

"Eleven days. That's not so long. Come on, now," she coaxed. "Be nice." She kissed him and pulled his ears and kissed him again and again until she got him to smile.

Being home was strange. It was good . . . and it was strange. "Gee, it's just the same," Nina said, walking from room to room. What had she expected? Was it that she herself felt so changed that she had thought her family would also be changed? But there was her father in the same slippers and baggy green work pants, still absorbed in the African violets he grew under purple lights in the kitchen. And there was her mother: the familiar, weary sweetness of her mouth; her rare smile. Her mother's eyes drew Nina: how dark they were! Reminiscently, Nina's own eyes lingered on the soft, dark pouches of skin beneath Shirley Bloom's eyes. As a small child Nina had loved to touch her mother's face, touch especially those dark, dark patches of skin.

"It's so nice to have you home again," her mother said almost shyly. "Just one person going out of the house makes such a difference. It felt empty for weeks."

"I didn't take up that much room, Ma!"

"Oh, Nina, I didn't say you did."

"Ma!" Nina hugged her. "You're as bad as me. I'm so naive. I never know when people are teasing me."

She examined herself in mirrors all over the house: speckled mirror in the bathroom, little oval mirror in the upstairs hall, long narrow glass over her parents' bulky, old-fashioned bureau. In every mirror she saw only herself. Nina Pudding Face. Her old disparaging name for herself popped out like a jack-in-the-box. Wasn't it awful? Without Mitch at her elbow to tell her he loved her, she fell right back into that old trap of disliking herself. She noticed that she was breathing with her mouth hanging open, a look she despised, a hangover from that year she'd had those terrifying I-can't-breathe attacks at night. The same year her father had had his heart operation. She shut her mouth, walked away from the mirrors.

"Hi, guys!" A big smile for her younger brothers who still stuck together like glue. "Remember me? I'm your sister." Billy looked disgusted. Eric rolled his eyes at her foolishness. "Don't recognize me, huh? I'm different, right?"

"Geez," Billy breathed. They ran past her.

"Dummy," Nina told herself. No wonder they wouldn't talk to her. Without thinking, she had adopted the same tone of jovial bullying her older brothers had always used toward her and all the younger ones. It seemed to her that she had never seen herself so clearly. It was as if by the act of going away and then returning home, she had split herself: she was still Nina, their Nina, but while she was joking up her brothers or teasing her mother or asking her father questions about his African violets, she was also, in a sense, outside herself, critically watching. Knew her teasing was designed to calm any suspicions her mother might have about how she was living. Knew she was pleasing her father with her questions.

In the morning, waking in her old bed, she stared at the ceiling, at the familiar cracks and water stains. The old house had many creaks, cracks, and groans. It was rarely silent. In the other bed, her first cigarette of the day dangling from the corner of her mouth, Nancy waved smoke out the partially opened window. "Does it smell in here?"

Nina turned on her side. "Good morning. You still trying to fool Mom about your smoking?"

"Betcha booties. Forget how she hates the weed? I don't know how she lived with Dad all those years before he gave it up."

"She's good," Nina said. The night before, looking at her mother as they all sat around the kitchen table eating dinner, Nina's heart had squeezed tight with passionate, ancient feelings: love, anger, pity, all fused together. "She's too good. Does she have to work so damn hard? She never stops. She's up before anyone— I hear her in the kitchen right now—and goes to bed after all of us."

"Did you come home to bring that news?"

Nina grimaced. Away from Nancy, she had been favoring her in her mind with a little glow, almost a halo. Her baby sister!

"Did Mom tell you Grandma's sick?" Nancy said.

"No."

"She's got cancer."

"I didn't know that! Is she in pain, Nan?"

"They've got her on drugs. She's still getting around and being pissy as ever to anyone who gets in her way. Remember what she used to say when I did something she didn't like? 'What dodo bird brought *you*?' I'd sass her back, then go in the closet in the hall and cry."

"Me," Nina said, "she used to grab by the shoulders. Hard."

"Yeah, well, she's not always the nicest old lady in the world. But I appreciate her more these days."

"She's dying?" Nina said. Hard to believe of that big woman with the work-roughened hands that could leave bruises on your shoulders.

"That's not why I appreciate her," Nancy said. "What I see with my own eyes is that not enough ladies, young or old, have got her vinegar running in their blood. So she's dying. Everybody dies. Anyway, she's eighty-three."

"Nancy, doesn't anything ever bother you?"

Nancy blew smoke to the ceiling. "Not if I can help it."

"How much do you smoke?"

"Couple packs a day."

"Aren't you worried about your health?"

"Why?"

"*Cancer.*" Nina wanted to dig beneath her sister's unflappable exterior.

"Well, I'll tell you," Nancy drawled. "I have a nasty fungus between my third and fourth toes, and last week I bashed a finger playing racquetball. But, otherwise, lungs included, I'm healthy as a horse. Which you have to be to work in the mill."

Nina heard that as a reproach. Nancy worked in the mill; *she* went to college. "I didn't know you played racquetball." But once again she was sitting on her own shoulder, watching, judging. Judging herself to be a fool to try to play Nancy's cool, cool game. *I didn't know you played racquetball.* What did that have to do with the way she was feeling, the things she was thinking?

"Guess you don't know a lot of things, Nina."

"You're right, Nancy," she said after a moment, "but I'm trying to learn."

"Go to it. Do your damndest." Everything Nancy said sounded faintly sardonic, as if she were forever having a huge private laugh at the world.

Nina's face flushed. They were back in their old groove—fencing. Nina says this . . . Nancy says that. Nina says thus and so . . . Nancy says yes and no. Fences going up, barriers of words stretching between them. And Nina had thought she would—*could*—talk to Nancy. Real talk. About Mitch—and love, and life. But they couldn't even talk about their grandmother.

"Is racquetball fun?" Nina said neutrally. "The professor I work for might teach me."

"Professors teaching racquetball? Some fancy college."

"Oh, we just live in the lap of luxury. Listen, Nance, do you ever think about college? It's not too late."

"No way, José. I made up my mind a long time ago to two things. One, I was getting out of school as fast as possible, never to return. And two, whatever I did, I would not spend my life stuck behind a desk typing up reports for a bunch of guys making more money than I ever could."

"So you like the mill?"

"I didn't say that. I like the girls I work with. I like the pay envelope every week. I like that part a lot."

"Any guys work there?"

"A few. They get the better jobs. Anything else you want to know?"

Nina could take only so much of this. Years ago she and Nancy had been friends, playing together, scrapping, sure, but a team, too—the only two girls in a family of boys. Where had it all gone? That pleasure of linked arms, of heads together, of climbing into the same bed at night, tenting the blankets and whispering plans for revenge on older, bullying brothers?

Nina's mother made the usual too-lavish Christmas Day dinner. The smell of roasting turkey and candied sweet potatoes filled the house. It snowed again. Had been snowing for days. Nina had almost forgotten how much snow fell in the foothills of the mountains. Every windowsill was thickly crusted with snow.

Her grandmother arrived with a huge pan of chestnut stuffing and three pies. "Let me see you, Nina." She put her hands on Nina's shoulders, and for a moment Nina felt seven years old again and on trial. Her grandmother's brown, bloodshot eyes stared into hers, and a guilty heat rose into Nina's cheeks. Did her grandmother know? Did she know that Nina was living with a man? *Living in sin*—that's what she'd call it. Nina forced herself to stand quietly.

"So . . . school is nice?"

"Very nice." Was that it? Was that all? Her grandmother's hands were not, she realized, gripping in the old, hard, unbearable way, but rather resting on her shoulders. Nina's heart galloped. She understood then that her grandmother was an old, sick woman. "I'm learning a lot, Grandma." She covered her grandmother's hands with hers.

The old lady's chins wobbled. "You're our smart one, Nina. You study hard. Don't be lazy!"

"Okay, Grandma." Standing on tiptoe, she kissed the leathery cheek.

The week passed slowly. Nina studied, tried to study; but time slipped away from her. She daydreamed, didn't get nearly as much done as she had planned. She called Mitch twice, but couldn't really talk—the phone was in the kitchen, and someone was always around. But after these conversations— hurried, muted, Mitch saying *I love you, come home, I miss you*—a great heat would creep into her belly; and later, in bed, lying facedown with her hands under her, she would imagine the two of them together again.

She slept a lot. Slept for hours and hours. "You're catching up with your rest," her mother said tenderly, as if she had a vision of Nina at college hunched over books into the small hours of every night.

On her last night home Nina found herself with Nancy in the kitchen, drinking beer and talking. "So you're going back tomorrow, and I didn't even ask you the big question," Nancy said. "How's the boyfriend situation?"

"Good enough," Nina said.

"Meaning?"

"Meaning—I've got a boyfriend."

"That's good?"

" 'Taint bad," she said, in Nancy's tones.

"Well, but—just one?"

"How many do I need? This one keeps me busy."

"Four would keep you busier." Nancy grinned, showing tiny baby teeth.

"Four?" Then Nina got it. "*You* have four boyfriends?"

Nancy ticked them off on her fingers. "Hugh, Mark, Bob . . . and sometimes Ed."

"Wow," Nina said inadequately.

"Well, life doesn't get boring that way, anyway."

"You like them all the same?" Nina tipped back in her chair, trying to take in Nancy. They were sisters, but so different. *She* was short, plump, a plugger (the mule); Nancy was needle-slender, light on her feet, a leaper and jumper. But none of that explained their differences.

Their relationship had been strained for some years now, probably since they'd gone into their teens. In high school Nancy had always had boys hanging around. Once Nina tried to talk to her, give her advice. She'd been playing Big Sister. Not for long. Nancy had cut her off, told her she, Nancy, knew more than Nina ever would. Maybe true. No maybes about it. True.

"Four guys," Nina said again. "Well, that must be . . . interesting."

"Yeah . . . inneresting," Nancy drawled. "Ever think of it? Ever think of going in for more than one at a time?"

"No . . . no. . . ." Nina said, and immediately thought of it. Mitch could be Numero Uno. After him, Nickiepie, then D.G. Or no, Adam, and *then* D.G. . . . She'd rotate them, give them each a week. . . .

She squinted at the beer bottle. Ha. She'd never be able to manage it. When she was with one, she'd be worrying about the other three. It wouldn't just take good organization. You needed a certain frame of mind. *Her?* She'd be covered with guilt and worry all the time. Imagine trying to keep four guys happy!

"I don't know how you do it," she said.

"Mark is my biggest problem. The guy wants to settle down. With me, believe it or not. He wants a little house, packs of kids—the whole bit. Okay for him, he's twenty-seven. But I'm still in my teens. I keep telling him, Go find yourself someone else, find yourself a nice little wifey, but he won't listen. Keeps hanging around. Insists he's going to reform me. He says it's natural for girls to want to get married and have kids. I told him, 'Yeah? Well, then I'm unnatural. It's my middle name. Nancy Unnatural Bloom.'"

Nina laughed. "So what does he say to that?"

Nancy shrugged. "The more I push him away, the closer he wants to get. Guys always want so much. Too much! I'm not getting tight with any one guy for a long, long time. And then I gotta find one who's different. Not possessive. Ever notice how they want you to be their chief possession? First it's *darling, sweetie, baby, honey,* and then they think they own you. You're supposed to be just grateful they love you."

"Well, maybe it depends on the person, the guy," Nina said mildly.

"It's a law of nature, Nina. Mighty hunter crap. They can't hunt down big game anymore, so they go after a woman. They're in their glory when they get you."

At once, uncomfortably, Nina imagined Mitch in a white safari suit standing with his booted foot on her prostrate rump. Geez! She put down her beer. Being around Nancy was catching.

"You serious with your guy?" Nancy asked.

"In a way, yes . . . definitely."

"He's in college, too, huh?"

"No, he does odd jobs for a company. Painting, kitchen work."

"You're kidding."

"He left college last year," Nina said, enjoying Nancy's astonishment. It wasn't often she could wipe that blasé look off Nancy's face.

"Why? Is he dumb?"

"Hey, Nan, everybody in college isn't a genius, and everybody out of college isn't a dope. Mitch happens to be a very smart person."

"Uh-huh," Nancy said with her little smile.

"Look," Nina said defensively, "he just didn't feel right about himself being in school. He said . . . he felt he didn't know that much about real life."

Nancy hooted, just as Nina had anticipated. "Send him down to the mill!"

"Well, that's more or less what he's doing for himself. He does all kinds of jobs . . . different work experiences. Right now he's laying tiles in a restaurant."

"Nina, for a smartie—" Nancy shook her head. "All these college hunks around, and you pick one that's laying tiles. I guess college isn't teaching you so much after all."

"I don't love him because of his job!"

"You *love* him? Even better. Nina, sometimes I feel like *your* big sister. Love, cookie, is a crock."

Nina leaned forward, pushing aside her beer bottle. "Nancy, you're not really that cynical."

"Yeah, I am. Is he sexy at least?"

"What do you think?" Nina said, stung.

Nancy laughed. "You're not going to like what I think. I think . . . how would big sister know what's sexy?"

Nina flushed. "I'm not that backward."

"Sure am glad to hear it. What does Tile Layer look like?"

"His name is *Mitch*."

"You getting mad?"

"Yeah!"

Nancy got two more bottles of beer. "Well, don't. It's just the way I am. We haven't had a good old girlie talk for years. Let's not blow it."

"You think it's my fault we haven't talked?" Nina asked stiffly.

Nancy shrugged. "I wouldn't say that. No, you're a lot more reasonable person than I am. A lot nicer, too; so I figure it's my fault—"

"Oh, stop. Why are you putting yourself down?"

"No, I mean it." She gave that milky-toothed smile that made her look about six years old. "I'm not putting myself down. Just—I know myself. And I don't hand out compliments much. Better take 'em when they come. You are a better person."

"And you're something else," Nina said.

"Compliment?"

"Yes!"

"Okay, thanks." Nancy smiled. "Let's be friends. It's kind of nice, isn't it?"

"It is; it is." Nina opened fresh bottles of beer and they each took a drink. "Nance? I want to tell you something." She drew closer, glanced at the closed door. "I don't want anyone else to hear—"

"You're not preggy!" Nancy said.

"Do you think I don't know anything?"

"What do you use?"

"The diaphragm," Nina said impatiently. "Listen—"

"I like the pill. I don't give a damn about those warnings. I think it's a great invention."

"Nance. I'm living with Mitch."

"You're living with the guy? You moved out of the place with those other girls?"

Nina nodded.

"Well, well, well. I never would've thought." Nancy chuckled. "*You're* something else."

"Do you think I should tell Mom?"

"Why?"

"Well . . . I don't like being deceitful. . . . Having secrets."

"Nina!" Nancy clutched her head. "Do not tell Mom."

"What if she comes up to visit me sometime and—"

"Oh, go on; she'll sooner take a walk on the moon. She's lucky she gets two miles down the pike once a week to play bingo at the American Legion Hall."

"I know, but . . . I feel guilty. It seems like I'm tricking her. I wish I could tell her, Nancy. Mitch is so wonderful. Why shouldn't she know?"

"Nina, the beer's getting to you! Why would you tell Mom? I'll tell you why. For your own sake! So you can feel all pure and uplifted. I cannot tell a lie, and all that junk. Don't kid yourself you'd be doing it for Mom, Nina. You'd be doing it for *Nina*. Listen, do you think I run around telling all?"

"That's different."

"What's so different? Gimme a break! I'm sleeping with my boyfriends, you're sleeping with your boyfriend. In a way, I think you living with this guy would be more upsetting to Mom than anything I do. I mean, I don't make my life public. I keep up a nice front for her and Grandma and everyone. And you should, too. I'll tell you something else. Mom's got big hopes pinned on you. All the things she never did, she's counting on you to do. You're the one who's going to graduate from college, get a nice job, and not rush into having kids too soon. Etcetera. If she knew you were living with Mitch, it would tear her up. She wouldn't say much, but she'd be thinking, There goes that. There goes my brilliant Nina, tied down and tied up."

"I'm not brilliant," Nina said in exasperation. "I wish you wouldn't keep saying that. If you knew how I beat my head against those books. If you knew how many smart people there are around, really smart. *You're* smarter than I am. Much smarter. And you know it, too."

"Since I'm so smart, listen to me, big sister. Do not tell Mom you're screwing around and—"

"I'm not *screwing* around, Nancy!"

"Oh, ho, I offended you? Okay, your highness, *I'm* screwing around, you're living in holy togetherness."

"Jesus, Nancy! That tongue of yours. Did you ever think you're a lot like Grandma?"

Nancy's mouth opened, then closed. She moved her beer bottle around and around in a wet spot. After a moment, she said, "You're right. I have a big mouth. It's my claim to fame." Her laugh sounded forced.

"Hey, Nance." Remorseful, Nina leaned across the table and took her sister's hand. "That was mean of me. A low blow. I'm sorry."

"Sure." Nancy shrugged, her eyes down.

"Don't be mad at me," Nina said. "Let's not throw this whole evening away. Nance—I'm really sorry."

Nancy nodded. "Well, Nina, it's just—I don't want you to hurt Mom. You probably forget what it's like around here. Everybody dumps on her. Me, too. She's kind of a saint, Nina. If there's anything I believe in," Nancy said in a low voice, "anything at all in this world, it's Mom. Well, you know what they say— ignorance is bliss. So I figure, let her be a little bit blissful."

They both fell silent. In the living room, they heard the sound of the TV. "Hey, how's old Emmett," Nancy said. "You still kiss him on the mouth?"

Nina smiled. "You and Mitch should get together. He can't stand it when I do that." She put the empty bottles on the floor. "Okay, Nance. You're right. I won't tell Mom about me and Mitch."

Chapter Sixteen

"Did you take my shoelace?" Mitch said.

"What?" Nina was in the kitchen, opening a can of cat food for Emmett.

"My *shoelace*. Did you take it?"

"Oh, right; I borrowed a lace from that boot you're going to have soled. One of mine broke—"

Mitch appeared in the doorway. "I didn't give you permission."

"Oh, pardon me, sir. My lace snapped, sir, and yours was handy, sir. . . ." Mitch wasn't laughing. Nina put down Emmett's dish. Could he be *serious*? Straightening up, she studied his face. "I didn't realize you were so fond of that particular lace. There it be—safe as houses." She gestured to her own boot.

"It would be nice if you asked before you took." His tone was aggrieved. Definitely not jokey.

"Mitch, you weren't using the boot. My lace broke and—"

"It's the principle of the thing, Nina. It's my shoe-lace. Out of courtesy you might have asked first before you grabbed."

Grabbed? "Well, I'm *sorry.*" Bending down, she yanked the lace out. "Here! It's all yours." She threw the lace at him and, with her shoe flapping, stalked into the other room. The trouble with stalking in this place was that you couldn't stalk very far. She got to the bathroom, hesitated, then, sensing his eyes on her, stalked in *there* and shut the door with a decisive take-that bang. In the bathroom, of course, there was even less space. She sat down on the rim of the tub, seething but without knowing quite what she was seething over. Had they had a fight, or not? A fight over a *shoelace?* This was ridiculous.

Suddenly she opened the door and yelled, "This is bloody ridiculous!" Then she slammed the door again.

She'd been back from her visit home for two days, and it seemed to her that they had had more stupid fights and pointless arguments in those two days than in all the preceding weeks. Had they really snapped at each other yesterday in the supermarket about which brand of baked beans to buy? And last night about the radio station Nina had tuned to? Good lord! She tapped her foot furiously. She had returned from her visit home full of expectations for their reunion, a kind of glory of rising music in her head. Reunion music. Bugles and sunrises and thudding hearts. Corny movie stuff, but there it was: she was excited, no, rapturous at the thought of seeing Mitch again.

He'd been waiting for her when she got off the bus. A thrill went through her, almost like the first time they'd really connected—that pang of recognition, that trembling in her stomach. She stopped dead still for a moment to look at him, just to take in the sight of him. On the grimy sidewalk, in the midst of all the people in their drab winter clothes with their weary winter faces, he glowed. A scarf was knotted loosely around his neck; his head was bare, and he'd had a haircut. Cut off all his curls! She stared, shocked. His hair was down to nearly a stubble. His eyes in that round skull were large and luminous.

She threw her arms around him. "You cut your hair!"

"You don't like it?" Then—how strange!—he'd smiled as if he hoped she *didn't* like this different-looking Mitch.

She had come back full of stories about home, Nancy, her brothers. She talked all the way to the apartment, glancing up now and then at his shaved head. Each time, a shock. Mitch listened to her, nodded, asked questions, but . . . something was wrong. Nina hung on his arm. Mitch allowed her to hang there. *That* was it. He *allowed* it. Allowed the hugs . . . allowed the kisses she planted on his face at every corner. She was wooing him, but no returns. Just that shaven head. "Well, that's enough about me." She kept it light, her voice cheery. Maybe she was imagining all this about his shaven head and his uncharacteristic reserve? "I really missed you." She hugged his arm. "I want to hear about you. Everything. Every detail," she had ordered.

"I went to work. Ate. Slept. Watched some TV. Read the newspapers. That's it. Nothing exciting. Nothing to tell, really."

"Sure there is. Must be. Did you see anything good on TV? Go to any movies? Did anybody call us? What about work? Did you phone your sister like you said you were going to?"

"Mmm. Called Trissy once, and then she called me a couple of days later."

"Terrific!" She sounded ridiculous, like a cheerleader. Yay, troops, you're doing *great*. Loud and cheerful even when they were losing the game. "Look," she said in a quieter voice, "are you all right?"

"Why not?" His eyes tilted away from hers. "You're back, aren't you?"

"I sure am!" The cheerleader again. "But my woman's intuition tells me something is not quite right."

He squeezed her arm. "Everything's fine." He changed the subject, said living near a college was unreal. "Where else do you have a neighborhood that the entire population suddenly deserts for two weeks? This whole shebang is like a ghost town. I should have moved a long time ago. I could probably get a much better place somewhere else for the same money."

"Leave the apartment?" A chill across her shoulders. Was he including her in the plans?

"We'll find another one."

All right, he said *we* . . . . Still, something amiss. She'd joked about her woman's intuition, but that was all she had to go on. A feeling. Sensing a shadow over his face even when he smiled.

Back in the apartment, he had turned on the radio, fidgeting with the dials. "So, how does everything look to you?"

"Great," she had said. A little messy, but so what? "How're we doing on food?" She investigated the refrigerator. "You know what, Mitch? I really missed shopping and cooking while I was home. Would you believe it? It was like a vacation—my mother did everything, but I kept thinking how we wouldn't have bought this or we would have bought more of that." She heard herself chattering. She picked Emmett up again for another long hug. "Was Fatty good? Did he bug you?"

"He was okay. We kept our distance from each other and got along respectably."

She went to clean the catbox. She had smelled it the moment she walked in. Phew. How did Mitch stand that? Holding out on that, too, until she returned. One chore he flatly refused to do, although he complained like hell if she let it go too long. Well, he'd cared for Emmett the whole time she was away. She wasn't going to say anything about the awful state of the box. That would definitely be ungracious— *ungrateful.*

Pouring fresh litter into the box, she had wondered if Mitch was resentful that he'd been left with Emmett.

Could that be it? It didn't occur to her then, nor did it occur to her as she sat on the rim of the tub, seething over the silly shoelace fight, that what he resented, what he was nursing like a wound, was that she had left him in the first place.

Chapter Seventeen

Lynell had also returned early to campus, and the three of them agreed to celebrate New Year's Eve together. That is, Mitch and Lynell agreed after talking on the phone the morning after the shoelace fight. *That* had never really been settled. Instead, they had both seemed to agree to let it drop. Nina had emerged from the bathroom, calmed down and determined to see the funny side of this business. "Safe to come out?" she'd asked. "Or am I about to be beaten with a shoelace?" Mitch laughed, looked relieved, and said, in a half apology, "I guess you never knew shoelaces could be a delicate subject."

Fine. That was that. But the next morning there was another difficulty. Hanging up after talking to Lynell, Mitch said, "We're picking up Lynell later when we go out." *Fait accompli.*

Nina had heard his end of the conversation of course. "Look, you can't stay alone on New Year's Eve. . . . No, don't be . . ." A pause, then "Come with *us*. Of course you won't be in the way!" And a moment later, another vigorous protest, "No, Nina won't mind."

Well, as a matter of fact, she did mind. She had thought New Year's, coming so soon on the heels of their separation, would be a special evening just for the two of them. Besides, there'd been so much tension in these few days, she'd hoped the whole process of dressing up and going out together would break the evil spell. It wasn't Lynell she objected to. It could have been Sonia. It could have been anyone, and she would have minded. But when Mitch told her Lynell was going out with them, Nina just nodded and said, "Sure, great." Well, what was she supposed to do? Stamp her foot? Refuse to go?

But she was disturbed. Mitch denied anything was wrong, but it was Nina's impression that by including Lynell, he was keeping a distance between them—that distance Nina had sensed ever since she returned. A distance he insisted was all in her imagination. But it was there. Oh, yes, it was *there*! Irritated with her over a shoelace? Come on! Absolutely, something was wrong; only she didn't have a clue to what it could be.

They met Lynell later that evening. "Mitch!" she exclaimed. "Your hair. You look like one of those handsome young punks from the fifties."

"You like it?"

"I love it!" Lynell linked arms with him.

"I'm still getting used to it," Nina said, smarting because she hadn't reacted with the same enthusiasm Lynell showed.

They walked down the street arm in arm. Snow fell. A hazy moon appeared on the horizon. "Would you believe it's warmer outside than in my apartment?" Mitch said.

Nina, suddenly sensitive to every nuance, heard that *my* and said, "It was so cold last night, our teeth chattered," just so she could say *our*.

"As friend D.G. would say, *literally* chattered?" Lynell shivered extravagantly in her down jacket and big fuzzy white mittens. "I believe it. Oh, take me back to sunny Cal."

"Well, we like winter, anyway," Nina said, getting in another *we*, and conscious of how silly this underground war—or whatever it was—was getting to be. A moment later she really regretted her proprietary remarks. Apparently nothing escaped Lynell.

"We?" Lynell said, smiling. "Love the way you say that, little Nina. Is that *we*, as in the royal *we*?"

Nina wished she had the nerve to tell Lynell to bloody cut out that little Nina stuff. *Just cut it out, Lynell! Stow it! Stuff it!*

They made the rounds of several places, drank, danced, and ended at midnight in a bar called the Green Rooster. The lights were dimmed. A feverish excitement leaped through the room. Bells rang. Screams and cheers. "Happy New Year! Happy New Year!" A horn blew, then another. Nina found herself being kissed by a guy with a red ponytail from the next table. He leaned over the space, grabbed her by the shoulders. "Happy New Year, doll." He smelled of cigarettes and beer and didn't want to let her go.

She turned to Mitch, who was kissing Lynell. A real kiss, she noted, not just a peck on the lips. Tapping him on the back, she announced, "Okay, my turn!"

They left the Green Rooster with Mitch between Lynell and Nina. "What now?" Lynell asked. "Are you guys going to flake out on me?" Drinking had put unaccustomed color into her normally pale cheeks.

They decided they would stay up all night and listen to John Lennon records in Nina and Mitch's place. In their apartment Nina put the records on the stereo while Mitch got a bottle of wine, crackers, and glasses. They sprawled on the bed, wrapping blankets around themselves. Thinking about John Lennon as his voice filled the room, tears came to Nina's eyes. Why should someone so young and talented have died? There was so much sadness in the world. Her grandmother was sick. Her father had been sick for years. Her mother worked too hard. And Nancy was stuck in a lousy factory job. She sniffled and wiped her nose on her sleeve.

"What's the matter, Nins?"

"I don't know. I just feel so sad." But at once she felt better. Mitch had noticed she was sad; his voice had been warm and caring. She hugged his arm and kissed his ear, wishing Lynell would go home.

"You shouldn't be sad on the New Year," Lynell said. "It's bad luck."

"She's a little smashed," Mitch said. And to Nina, "You get smashed so easy, honey."

"I know," she sniffled. "I'm sorry, I can't help it."

Emmett climbed into her lap, and Nina dried her face on his fur.

Soon Lynell and Mitch got into an argument about the difference between truth and nastiness in John Lennon's music. "Nastiness—I'd even call it malice—was an integral part of his art. . . ."

"All his songs aren't nasty. How can you say that?"

"Now, listen to what I'm saying. I didn't mean all his songs, but when you examine the lyrics—"

Nina didn't want to examine the lyrics. She just wanted to listen to the music and *feel* it. There were times when she didn't understand what some of the words meant, but the song still swept through her. That was enough for her. Long before either Mitch or Lynell gave up on their argument, Nina, bored and sleepy, yawning uncontrollably, pulled a blanket over her shoulders and fell asleep. Some time later, she was vaguely aware of Mitch getting in next to her.

In the morning, when she woke up, she saw Lynell, covered with a quilt, sleeping on the couch. Her hair fanned out around her shoulders. Her jeans and shirt were on the floor.

Nina's eyes ached, the inside of her mouth was dry and pasty. An unpleasant thumping started in the back of her head. Damn. A hangover. She stared at Lynell, curled up, her mouth slightly parted; stared at the heap of clothes on the floor. She smelled the light perfume Lynell used. Emmett climbed up on her stomach. She pushed him away. "I'm not in the mood now, Emmett!"

Chapter Eighteen

The room is dark, lit only by the glow from the street. Arms twined around each other's necks, foreheads pressed together, Nina and Mitch dance slowly between the furniture, slow, shuffling steps interspersed with long kisses. Dancing . . . humming . . . stumbling into a chair, catching each other. . . . Giggling, then more shuffling, slow steps around the table . . . to the door . . . past the big old chair. "Dancing in the daaark . . ." Mitch sings in her ear.

This is the good time, the perfect time. So fine, so fine and good, so much better than the—well, not so good times. The times when they fight, when they irritate each other, when things, for no reason, go sorrily wrong. Like the morning after the night Lynell slept over. New Year's Eve—weeks ago, but Nina still thinks about it now and then, thinks how unpleasant it was waking up with someone else in their room. What she really remembers: the fragrance of Lynell's hair filling the air. How it irritated her. And how, as soon as Lynell left, she and Mitch had a huge fight over something so inconsequential, two hours later she couldn't remember what it was that set them off. A not so good time.

And another not so good time just this morning. Not so many hours ago. Stupid little quarrel. Silly, stupid, awful quarrel . . . starting over nothing again, over breakfast, over Nina's not wanting to sit down and eat. *I don't have time, Mitch. I want to get to the library.*

Please sit down at least to drink your coffee, Nina. You drive me crazy, pacing up and down.

Okay, okay! No, I can't. I didn't feed Emmett yet.

He can go without a meal once in a while. He could live off his fat for a month.

Oh, come on! How'd you like it if someone said you didn't need your breakfast? Anyway, I don't want to argue about Emmett.

Good. Sit down and eat like a human being.

Would you please lower your voice? You're yelling, Mitch.

Not exactly whispering yourself, Nina.

Oh, for . . . ! Look, let me feed Emmett and—

Emmett, Emmett. You ever think about anything but Emmett?

Jealous of a cat, Mitch? Don't tell me that!

Sick, Nina. That cat is no more than a bug to me. I could step on him and squash him without a thought.

The remark stuck in her belly, grew, swelled. She went away from the table, came back a moment later, her face blazing. *I didn't like that crack about Emmett.* Slapped Mitch on the arm for emphasis. He slapped her back across the cheek. Then slapped her again. Stunned, she didn't respond. *Come on, fight back,* he ordered.

No. She had screamed. *No.*

"Dancing in the daaark . . . with youuuuu . . ." Emmett howls painfully.

"He doesn't like your voice." They giggle. Emmett doesn't bother them. Nothing bothers them. They are in harmony once again. A single voice. "Dancing in the daaark . . ." they sing together.

All day she'd been miserable, thinking about their quarrel in the morning. As soon as he came home from work, she had gone to him. *I'm sorry I hit you this morning. I shouldn't have done that. I started the whole thing, but you know how crazy it makes me when you get on Emmett's case.* He'd put out his arms to her right away. *I was terrible. I don't know what got into me. I got so mad when you socked me. I just reacted, Nins.*

I hated you when you slapped me!

I've been hating myself all day.

They dip past the table; Mitch reaches out, picks up a glass of wine, sips, holds it to Nina's mouth. . . .

They kiss again. . . . Again. . . . The wine tastes sweet on their sticky lips. . . . Sweet . . . how sweet to hold each other this way, to lean dizzily toward each other. Doubly sweet in the aftermath of a fight.

"Oh, Mitch . . ."

"Oh, Nina . . ."

Names whispered like icons . . . tokens . . . blessings. This is love, Nina thinks. This is love.

Chapter Nineteen

Swinging the racket Professor Lehman had lent her, Nina charged after the little blue ball. She wiped her forehead. She was sweating furiously, but Nicholas Lehman looked as cool and fresh as when they entered the court. He was wearing a red shirt and a red bandanna around his forehead. Very dashing. "Eye on the ball, Nina," he called, "not the racket."

"I know, I know," she muttered between her teeth. It annoyed her that she wasn't picking up this game faster. He stopped her as she started to swing overhand. "Wait. Not that way." Standing behind her, he held her hand and simulated the stroke. "Lots of wrist and hit low, otherwise you lose power."

They began again. He tapped the ball to the front wall. She returned it. He hit it back to her, and so on.

He kept calling out encouraging remarks. "You're doing it, Nina. . . . Good! . . . That's the way. . . ." In her eagerness to make a shot, she ran full tilt into him. "Sorry. Sorry!" The contact excited and embarrassed her.

"No problem." He steadied her. "Ready?" He hit the ball to the front wall. "Remember, hit it low, Nina."

She swung and, for the first time, racket and ball made solid contact. *Thwack!* "Wow," she said. "I think I did it right that time."

"You sure did. That's a great feeling, isn't it?"

There was a loud knock on the court door. The next players claiming their time. "How do you feel?" Nicholas Lehman asked Nina as they walked off.

"My legs are a little wobbly. They feel like spaghetti or something."

"Well, you'll build up stamina."

"I really appreciate your teaching me, Professor Leh—"

"Make it Nicholas," he said. "We're not in the classroom now." He tugged one of her braids. "You did okay. You did fine."

She took a long, hot shower and dressed slowly. As she left the gym a pale winter sun was going down behind the music building with its long churchy windows, and the bare black branches of maple trees were silhouetted against a silvery sky. She stopped for a moment to look at the sky. Her hair was damp, her cheeks still hot from the game. Then, hurrying, thinking about Mitch, she raised an imaginary racket and cocked her wrist. She would certainly brag a little to Mitch.

"Mitch?" She opened the door, toed Emmett in. "Back, baby. Hi, Mitch," she yodeled, "I'm ho-oome."

He came out of the kitchen. "Hi, where've you been?"

"Wait till you hear." She dropped her knapsack.

"It's late. I couldn't figure out where you were. It's your turn to make supper."

"Oops." In the kitchen Nina opened a can of tuna fish, tore apart a head of lettuce, and sliced a tomato. Bread, mayo, and cold baked beans from the night before. "Did you eat anything? Chow's ready." She set dishes on the table, shoving aside books and newspapers.

Emmett got up on his hind legs, pawing the edge of the table. He smelled the tuna fish.

"Nina, I'm going to lock him in the bathroom if you can't control him."

She pushed Emmett's paws off the table. "Guess where I was."

"Just tell me, will you? I'm not in the mood for games."

"What's the matter, Mitch?" She looked at him closely. "Are you okay?"

"Nina, you're always here when I get home from work. I was worried."

"Oh. I'm sorry! But you didn't have to worry."

"I can't help it. You can't just go dancing around these streets any old time of the night. It's dark out and—"

She laughed at him and waved her fingers at her temples. "Boo!"

He didn't laugh back. "I still don't know where you were. Working?"

"Better than that! Playing racquetball. You should have seen me, Mitch. Professor Lehman said if I kept at it, I had the makings of a strong player."

"You were playing with him?"

"Right! Remember he promised to teach me the game? I thought he forgot all about it, but he didn't. Today, he said, did I still want to learn, and I said, Sure! Mitch, at first I was so klutzy! Then, just at the end, I really got it. I hit the ball right. Know what I mean? *Smacko!* I was so proud of myself. Mmm, I was wonderful!" She ran kisses up her arm.

"Christ, Nina, is everything funny to you? I was worried about you."

"I'm sorry, Mitch; I really am. I didn't think you'd worry."

"Right. You didn't think."

"I said I was sorry."

"You're never late."

"All right. For the last time, I'm *sorry*. Let's not make a federal case out of this."

"Oh, the hell with it." He left the table.

She chewed a mouthful of baked beans. Ugh. Cold and hard and sicky sweet. She spit them out onto her plate. She'd come home in such a good mood, and now it was spoiled. Mitch had spoiled it. And why? What had she done? What crime had she committed? There he sat, in the big chair, turning the pages of a magazine as calmly as if he hadn't whipped up this whole storm over nothing. She gave him an evil look. He turned another page, cleared his throat. Acted as if she weren't even there. Nasty! She couldn't stand the silence. "Let's have it out," she said, jumping up. "You're jealous, aren't you, Mitch? That's what's bugging you! Come on, Mitch, admit it! You weren't worried about me! Just stupid jealous."

"You're screaming," he said without looking up.

"Hell!" She knew that bit. She'd heard all about how in his family they *never* screamed. Well, they didn't scream in *her* family, either, but they could make a little noise when the occasion demanded. She slapped one of their folding chairs together.

Mitch threw down the magazine. "Okay, Nina, okay." He went to the closet and pulled on his jacket.

"What are you doing?"

"Going out. Obviously it's not going to be very pleasant here."

"Running away," she accused. "Right? Running away! If we're going to fight, let's fight and get it over with."

He went to the door. She ran after him, planted herself in front of him, blocking the door. "I don't want you to go, Mitch. I want to have this out here and now. You're jealous, and you don't have any reason to be. It's just plain unfair and stupid."

"Will you cut out that jealous crap!" His mouth was tight, his brown eyes almost muddy with anger.

"Oh, but it's true. You can't stand that Nicholas—"

"Nicholas?"

Her face heated. "He said, since we weren't in class, I should call him—"

"Nicholas!" Shoving her aside, he yanked open the door. Did he mean just to push her? To move her out of the way only enough to get to the door? He pushed hard—hard enough to be called a shove, and she fell back, smacking her head against the wall. Tears sprang to her eyes. Mitch went out, and Emmett, skulking around the door as usual, followed him. For an instant, stunned, Nina didn't move.

Then, "Emmett!" she cried. "Come back here, Emmett." Hearing her voice, he flattened himself to the floor. Nina ran into the hall and scraped him up; he hung in her arms, resigned dead weight.

In the apartment, she went to the window and looked down into the street. A car spun its tires in the snow. The pink neon light from the record shop blinked hypnotically. Mitch was nowhere in sight. She turned away from the window. God, how depressing the room was with the bed unmade, clothes piled everywhere, and the table covered with books and half-eaten food. The back of her head began to ache.

She sat down with her books to study, but she couldn't concentrate. One summer, years ago, after a picnic at Cranberry Lake, her father had bought everyone presents. A green, sweet-smelling pillow for her mother with "I Pine for You and Balsam, Too," stitched on it in white; toy hatchets for the little boys, Ranger Rick hats for the big ones; and a birch bark canoe for her and Nancy. At home they had tied ribbons around two twigs, named them Fancy and Fina, and sent the brave girl explorers off in the canoe to paddle through tidal waves, whirlpools, and tropical storms they whipped up in the bathtub. Fancy and

Fina to the rescue of shipwrecked sailors and ladies endangered by ferocious crocodiles.

One day as they knelt in front of the tub, the canoe sprang a leak and sank. Nina, amazed and furious, had cried, "It was supposed to float forever!"

Now Nina imagined herself and Mitch in that canoe. Was water already seeping in? Were they in danger of sinking? Or were they already sunk? Was that what tonight's fight meant? But they'd fought before, plenty of times. And made up every time. What was different about tonight? Two things. One— Mitch's shoving her. Again she touched the back of her head. It wasn't that he'd hurt her so much. What hurt more than her head was the way he'd walked out. And that was the second different thing—that he'd run away from their fight instead of entering into it.

"Damn it, Mitch, come back!" she said suddenly in such a loud voice that Emmett scooted under a chair.

When he did return about an hour later, Nina was in bed, studying.

"Hello," he said, taking off his jacket.

"Hello."

They eyed each other. He glanced at the remains of food on the table. "It was your turn to clean up," Nina said.

"Oops." He grinned hopefully at her.

Hard to resist that, but she worked at it.

He sat down at the foot of the bed, pushing his hands through his hair, which had mostly grown in again. "I found out today that I might get laid off the job. They're short of work right now, and I'm one of the newest workers. Low man on the totem pole." He fiddled with the edge of the blanket. "I guess that's why I was so jumpy tonight. I was going to tell you about it, and then you didn't come home and—"

"I'm very sorry to hear you might be laid off."

"Sarcasm?"

"Can't I say *anything* without—"

"Well, you sounded sort of sarcastic. You didn't sound sorry."

Nina looked at him neutrally. "You're not actually laid off?"

"No, it was just . . . All the guys were talking about it, and—"

"You get jumpy real easily."

"Now, *that* was sarcasm."

She shrugged. They looked at each other.

"How about kissing and making up?" he said, leaning toward her.

She drew back slightly. "You know, you shoved me. I hit my head on the wall. You shoved me pretty hard."

He looked down. "Does it hurt?"

"Yes. . . ."

"Much? Where? Here—?" He touched the back of her head.

"Ouch!"

"It hurts that much?"

"You think I'm making it up? And something else —Emmett almost got out!"

"You got him back, all right, though."

"No thanks to you. . . . Mitch, I don't like your jealousy. That was it, wasn't it? Not the job, really. Just jealousy."

He was looking more and more miserable. "I'm sorry, Nina," he said in a low voice.

She grabbed the blanket in both hands. No satisfaction in this! "Listen, let's just forget it, okay? You're sorry. I'm sorry. So we're even!" Her throat tightened. It was a lot easier to be angry when it was clear he was at fault, but with him standing there looking abject . . . And she heard how she sounded—bitchy, mean, ungenerously not letting him make up with her. "Maybe we'll both feel better in the morning," she said, sliding down under the covers. Damn. She didn't want to cry.

"Are you coming to bed?" she said in a stiff, hoarse voice.

He dropped his clothes, shut the lights, and crawled in next to her. After a long time of lying very still and being careful not to let her arm or leg touch his, she sighed deeply. At once he said, "Are you sleeping?"

"No."

"Sleepy?"

"I don't know. No. . . ."

"Thinking?"

"A little. . . ."

"What are you thinking about?"

She sighed again and said in a muffled voice, "Not much. Just feeling sad mostly."

"About us?"

"Mmm. . . ."

Another silence. Then he said, "Want me to tell you a story?"

"A *story*?"

"Funny story. It'll make you laugh."

"I wish something would."

He leaned on his elbow, his face above hers. "Okay, there were three male ants and one female ant stuck in a jar. The first male ant says to the female ant, 'Wanna get out of this jar?' So she says, 'I sure do, but I don't know how.' 'Well,' he says, 'sleep with me tonight, and I'll tell you how in the morning.' But in the morning he's gone, and she's still stuck in the jar. So the second male ant says, 'Want to get out of this joint?' And she says, 'Yes! But I don't know how.' And he says, 'Well, look, sleep with me tonight, and I'll tell you how in the morning.' So she does. But comes the morning, and he's gone, too, and she's still in the jar. Well, along comes the _third_ male ant, and the same thing happens all over again. It's morning and all three male ants are gone, and there she is, still in the jar."

"That's very interesting," Nina said. "Sort of true to life. But funny?"

"I'm not through yet." His face in the light from the street was brighter, the drawn look gone. "Patience, please. Anyway, as I said, all three male ants are gone, and she's stuck in the jar. _But_ . . . the next morning, she's gone, too! Want to know how she got out?"

"Okay, I bite. How'd she get out?"

He paused for a moment, then said, "Sleep with me tonight, and I'll tell you in the morning." Nina bit back a smile. "Aha, that's funny, isn't it?" Mitch said.

"Cute," she admitted.

"Funny."

"Well . . ."

"Come on, Ms. Bloom Bloom, where's your sense of humor?"

"Okay, funny."

"Mean it?"

"Yes, you dog!"

Mitch winced. "Do you hate me? Do you hate me for what I did, Nina?"

"No, I don't *hate* you."

"Do you like me?"

"Mmm . . . usually."

"How about right now?"

"Well . . . I like you more than I did five minutes ago."

"Nina . . ." Tentatively, he kissed her. Then kissed her again. In a moment he said, "Are we okay now?"

She held him tightly. She was crying. How crazy to cry now when they were making up. She couldn't stop. Held him and cried . . . cried and cried and cried.

Chapter
Twenty

"You had change yesterday," Mitch said.

"I must have spent it all." Nina checked her pockets again. Usually the Laundromat was full on Saturday morning, but they had come in early, and it was empty except for them. "I'll go across the street and get change in the Record Shack."

"All those stores are closed until ten," Mitch said. Did he have to look so morose? Not having change wasn't exactly the end of the world. "I told Kenny we'd meet at the gym at nine thirty."

"You can meet Kenny. I'll do the laundry."

"We should have had change with us."

He didn't say it was her fault, but that was what she heard in his voice. Why was it her responsibility? He could have saved his quarters. With an effort she held her tongue. All week he'd been teetering on the edge of a mood. Waking up in the morning and staring at the ceiling, rubbing his cheek, rubbing and rubbing as if he were intent on rubbing off a layer of skin. "You realize it's March?" she'd said this morning. "Winter's almost over. Yay! Yay!"

He'd smiled, but it was a forced little smile. "Mitch" —she had leaned up on her elbow—"is something bothering you?"

He shook his head.

"You're so quiet lately," she persisted.

"No . . . not really. Just thinking about things." And he got out of bed and went into the bathroom. Shut the door to the bathroom. Shut the door on her, as well. *Thinking* about things? Well, maybe . . . but, if so, it was at least partially to find stuff to pick on about her. The other day it had been her old gray cords that she'd had forever. "How come you wear such baggy pants?" he asked. They were her most comfortable pants, but she changed to another pair. Maybe she was making a mistake being so obliging. The next day it was something else—the sugar she used in her coffee.

"You just dump it in, Nina. You're giving yourself a sugar high. Which means you've got to come down, maybe crash. That low feeling in the middle of the day. . . . Why don't you try drinking your coffee black?"

As if he didn't eat a glazed doughnut almost every single morning. "I'll try to take less," she said shortly. She liked her coffee sweet.

Then there'd been the business with the tights. Well, in that case he hadn't exactly dumped on her. Or should she say dripped? What happened was that, as usual, in the evening she'd washed out her tights, a new deep-purple pair, and hung them over the shower bar to dry. Two minutes later Mitch was in the bathroom, muttering about fixing the leaky cold water faucet in the tub. It had been leaking for weeks, and nobody, including the super, including Mitch, had seemed to care. But suddenly he had to stop that faucet from dripping. Now. This minute. "I'm sick of hearing the blasted thing drip drip drip."

He sat down on the rim of the tub right underneath her dripping wet tights. Naturally they dripped on him. What a cry he let out! As if he'd been wounded instead of merely wetted. "Oh, Mitch." Nina's sympathy lasted only a second. Streaks of purple dye streamed down his cheeks. She started to laugh. The wrong thing to do!

"Damn it, Nina . . . your stupid tights . . . could have told me. . . . Blah blah blah. . . ." His cheeks swelled, his eyes were moist, his lips puffed out. He reminded Nina of a huge baby in jeans and work boots having a little tantrum. An unfortunate image —it made her laugh harder.

"I'm sorry," she kept saying. "I'm sorry, Mitch . . . Only you . . . your face . . . look at yourself . . . ! Ha ha ha . . ."

Well, he'd gotten *his* back this morning, just before they'd come out with the laundry. "You're breathing with your mouth open," he said as they left the apartment. "You sleep that way, too. Your mouth hanging open."

A real surprise attack. It sounded as if she were the village idiot. She cringed. Wasn't he the one who said it was cute the way she mouth-breathed?

Then, as if all that didn't hurt enough, he had snapped her mouth shut with the flat of his hand.

Not a good start to the morning. And now . . . he was looking at her as if by not having coins for the machines she'd goofed on a matter of national security. She dropped the laundry bag. "I'll go get some change," she said flatly. She went outside and saw at once he was right—the stores were closed. She looked around.

"Pardon me, do you have change for—" A woman in a red ski hat brushed Nina aside as if she were an insect. Was that the kind of day it was going to be _all day_? Next she tried a man. "Change?" he said. "Sure. Come right over here." He pointed to a doorway with an obscene gesture.

"Oh, bug off," Nina said wearily. She rubbed her arms. It was one of those raw, not-quite-winter, not-yet-spring days. An old man approached. "Would you have change for a couple dollars?" she asked, deciding that after this the laundry could rot. She wasn't going to ask anyone else.

"I might, I might." He gave her a sunny smile, showing big, white, false teeth.

"I need quarters for the Laundromat," she said, "or I wouldn't bother you."

He pulled a black purse out of his pocket. His hands were spotted with brown liver marks. "Let me see . . . I have a penny, no, two pennies . . . a nickel here, and here we have one quarter." He held a quarter up between fingers that trembled slightly. "Now, let's see what else we have. Don't get impatient, young lady. Plenty of time." And again that sunny smile. "Is someone waiting for you?"

"My boyfriend."

"He'll wait, he'll wait." He was wearing a Windbreaker and a wool hat pulled down over his ears. "Why wouldn't he wait for a nice girl like you? Oh, ho, what's this?" He pulled out two more quarters. "You see! Isn't it a good day? Looks like we'll see another spring yet, and that's something, isn't it? Aha, more quarters. Here—no, no, you hold these while I look for the last one, and then you can give me the bills." He dipped his skinny fingers into the purse again.

"I'm really sorry to bother you," Nina said.

"It's a pleasure. Here I am talking to a pretty young girl and thinking, What can I tell her to impress her? Can you guess how old I am?"

"Ahh, seventy-five?"

"Eighty-four," he said.

"Really! That's wonderful."

"Eighty-four," he said again. "I wouldn't lie to you. What for? I can't stand these old duffers who lie to build themselves up. Have a little modesty is what I say."

"My grandmother is eighty-three," Nina said.

"And still enjoying life, I suppose. Here we are, patience rewarded." He handed her the last quarter.

"Well, thank you, really," Nina said. "You're very

nice." Impulsively she kissed him on the cheek.

"Well! Thank *you*." He pulled off his wool cap and bowed.

In the Laundromat Mitch was slumped by a window, hands in pockets. "Mitch, you'll never guess . . ." Nina put her arm around his waist. "I met the nicest old man!" Mitch blinked at her, a muzzy, faraway look, as if he'd been asleep on his feet. "Are you all right?" she asked involuntarily, thinking she was saying that a lot lately.

"Oh . . ." He straightened up, pushed his hands through his hair. "Let's do the laundry."

"Yes, let's," she said tightly, all at once as blue and discouraged and as near tears as Mitch had seemed last night when her tights dripped purple dye on him.

"Nina? Mitch? Hi." Lynell put her head into the apartment. Sunday afternoon. Outside it was raining snow. Nina, her books spread out on the table, was trying to draw conclusions for a paper from a statistical analysis of the weight and height of children between the ages of one and ten who were institutionalized, compared to a similar group of children raised in their own homes. She was also trying to ignore Mitch, who, perched on the windowsill, had been wheeling a red yo-yo up and down for the last hour. Up and down. Up and down. He wasn't bothering her. He'd been quiet. He wasn't even playing the radio. That was the trouble. It was unnatural for him to be so quiet. Not a word out of him. Just the red yo-yo moving up, moving down.

How could you love someone and still feel so exasperated with him? Contrary impulses had her mumbling under her breath. She wanted to kiss him and shake him at the same time. Wanted to be nice and also shout in his ear. *Come on, baby, get out of those blues! Look at me! Give me a kiss! Let's make love!* Yes, let's make love. She'd been sure they would this morning. Sunday morning. A good morning to hang out in bed, cuddle, and love each other. A good morning to make up for the past draggy week. But instead, Mitch had been up with the birds and out for the Sunday paper, and before the yo-yo got him in its spell, he'd spent two hours on the floor, with the paper spread out, reading it from front to back. Nina could swear he hadn't skipped a word, not even the pages of small print classified ads.

"I brought your mail, Nina." Lynell hovered in the doorway.

"Well, come on in." What was the matter with Lynell? Why so hesitant? So un-Lynellish? Was the whole world out of orbit? Or was it her?

"It's stifling in here." Lynell pulled off a heavy maroon ski sweater. Underneath she was wearing a white embroidered blouse, tight-fitting jeans, and lots of silver around her neck. "Hello, Mitch."

"Hello, Lynell." He smiled faintly. "Want me to open a window?"

"Sure. Okay with you, Nina?"

"Go ahead."

Nina and Lynell watched as Mitch heaved up the window. A puff of cool, moist air moved through the room. Something else moved through the room, something unseen but felt—an indefinable current. Nina wound her legs around the chair. Lynell seemed downcast, her smooth, small features a little pinched. "How's everything, Lynell?"

"Oh, tra la la."

"What does that mean? Good or bad?"

"Depends on your point of view. Adam and I had a fight."

"For real?"

"About as real as it could be. A biggie. We've packed it in."

"You broke up? When did that happen?"

"Oh . . . about a week ago."

"I'm sorry, Lynell."

"Don't be. It had to happen. I wasn't about to go on forever being one of his many women."

"You mean—more than that girl in Michigan?"

"Well, as a matter of fact, yes. Turns out he has some girl in Washington who is also crazy about him. I told him, he's like a sailor with a girl in every state."

"He had three girl friends?" Nina said.

"At least," Lynell said. "Don't look so shocked."

"I am. Adam . . . I liked him."

"Sure, you did, that's the point! Every girl he laid eyes on liked him! The whole thing went on too long. I should have kissed him off a long time ago. My mistake! I asked him, 'Are you going to miss me?' And he said, 'Yes.' I said, 'How much?' He said, 'A lot.' That's what I wanted to hear." She drummed her fingers on the arm of the chair. "Oh, that greedy greedy punk!"

The phone rang. Mitch answered, and Lynell went

to the stereo and put on a record. It was unfamiliar to Nina. "It's Rampal playing Telemann's Fantasies for Flute," Lynell said to her inquiring look. The clear, pure notes filled the room.

"Pretty," Nina said.

"Pretty?" Lynell sat down cross-legged on the bed. "If I could ever play the flute like Rampal, I don't think anything else would matter. Including men."

"For you, Nina," Mitch said, beckoning her to the phone.

"He's a master. A genius," Lynell said.

Nodding respectfully, Nina picked up the phone. "Hello?"

"Nina? Hello, it's Nicholas Lehman. Could you possibly come into the office this afternoon to do some typing?"

"Today?"

"I know," he said apologetically. "I hate to ask on a weekend, but I have something I'd really like to get off in the mail first thing tomorrow morning."

"All right. Sure. I'll be there in about twenty minutes."

"Who was that?" Mitch said as she hung up.

"Professor Lehman. He wants me to do some typing."

"It's Sunday, Nina. You don't have to work on Sunday."

"I know, but it's sort of an emergency."

"Call him back, tell him you can't make it. Let's go out. Let's do something—the three of us."

Nina stood irresolute for a moment, then shook her

head. "I already said I'd come in, Mitch. I won't be long. Probably not more than an hour." She pulled a scarf over her head and went to the door.

Mitch threw out the yo-yo, then snapped it back. "Suit yourself. Lynell and I will keep each other company. We can cry on each other's shoulders."

"I could use a nice crying shoulder," Lynell said as Nina went out the door.

Chapter Twenty-one

All through that last week of March the weather was raw, rainy, and windy. Not pleasant, but bearable. Then overnight winter returned, and in the morning, on WYUR, Stormy the Weatherman announced with a note of distinct pleasure, "We're having a real winter situation, folks, with below-freezing temperatures and lots of snow activity."

"Winter again?" Nina said. "Blaaaagh!"

"Who's afraid of Old Man Winter?" Grabbing Nina around the waist, Mitch danced her wildly around the room.

"Mitch-ell! Stop, you idiot." After narrowly missing Emmett and then a mess of boots and books in the middle of the floor, they came to rest against the door.

"You are nuts." Nina pinched his cheek. "I like you, nutso."

"Do—do—do you, Nina?" Abruptly his mood changed. He took her hands. "Do you like me?" His eyes were a little bloodshot; he'd had a cold for the past few days.

"Mitch—I love you." He'd—thank goodness!—come out of his glooms, but he still fell into long moments of brooding and sometimes—it was startling —his usual confident speech was replaced with a kind of stammering hesitation. "Do you?" he said again.

"Do *you*? Do you love me?"

"What do you think?"

"Yes . . . but I like to hear you say it."

"I wouldn't be here if I didn't," he said. The color in his face deepened.

"You're blushing," Nina said. Why was it so touching to see a man blush? "I didn't know you blushed."

"I didn't know it, either." He looked at himself in the mirror over the bureau. "I am not. You're making it up, Bloom."

"No, you are. Look at yourself! Know what my grandmother used to say? 'Blushing like the rosy dawn.' "

"Grandma sounds like a poet." He shoved Emmett off a chair and sat down to lace up his boots.

"You wouldn't say so if you met her. She has all these sayings. Hard work never hurt anyone. A stitch in time saves nine. What dodo bird brought you? Look before you leap, etcetera, etcetera. Did you see my keys?"

"On the bureau. Unless Emmett knocked them off. I never heard that one about the dodo bird. What does that mean?"

"That's the Nancy special." They left the apartment together, still talking.

When she went to work in Nicholas Lehman's office later that day, the place was a mess. During the night the pipes that ran across the ceiling had frozen and burst. There were puddles of water on the floor, and everything on the desk was drenched. "Look at this, Nina." He showed her a pile of smeared yellow pages. "All my latest notes. Not more than a sentence here and there intact. I'm going to have to reconstruct everything."

"I'm so sorry," she said.

"Well . . ." He sighed. "No use crying over spilt milk."

Nina couldn't help smiling. "That's one of the things my grandmother is always saying."

He nodded. "Until they get this office cleaned up, no use even trying to work here. I've got an office in my house. We'll use that. It's not far from here." He scribbled directions for her to his house on Elm Place. Nina said she'd show up the next day, at the usual time.

"Good, I'll be there," he said, again flipping through the pad of useless notes.

With no work, Nina was on her way home early— and just as well. She'd been having cramps all afternoon, and on this dismal, cold, snowy afternoon she was looking forward to climbing into bed with a hot water bottle and a cup of steaming tea. Later, when Mitch came home, maybe they'd watch TV together while they ate supper.

Her key was turning in the lock when she heard voices inside. Only the week before, two apartments on the first floor had been robbed in the middle of the day. "Who's there?" she said, banging on the door. Was that smart? She backed off, preparing to run, when the door opened and Mitch looked out. "Nina?"

"Oh, Mitch! You scared the life out of me." She toed Emmett back into the apartment. "I thought you were a thief."

"Hi," Lynell said. She was standing by the window.

"Hi," Nina said, surprised. What was Lynell doing here? Come to think of it, what was Mitch doing home so early? She put down her knapsack, taking out Mitch's mail and the bag of kitty litter she'd bought on the way home. "What's happening?" she said. There was a cardboard pizza box on the table. "It is Thursday, isn't it? Not Saturday?" She was woozy, as if her belly cramps had gone to her head and were distorting all her perceptions.

"Thursday," Lynell said.

"Thursday," Mitch agreed.

Nina blinked at their Bobbsey Twins act. Everything seemed slightly off balance: that strange sensation that comes when you walk into an empty room where a chair rocks, a curtain flutters. Whose body rocked the chair? Whose hand fluttered the curtain? Ghosts?

Lynell and Mitch hardly looked ghostlike. Really, just the opposite. Mitch's lips struck Nina as especially full and red, and Lynell, who was usually a little pale, almost gleamed with color. A raspberry blouse, kelly-green slacks, and a bright green polka-dotted band tied around her forehead.

"Mitch and I ran into each other and started arguing about the concert the other night," Lynell said. "We came up to finish our argument and eat pizza."

"I didn't go," Nina said.

"I know. You should have. The soprano was good and—"

"More than good," Mitch said. "She was impressive."

"You went?" Nina said to Mitch. "I thought you were playing basketball at the center with Kenny."

"No, I told you—"

"I thought you were playing basketball," Nina said again.

"Didn't you notice she had pitch problems at the top?" Lynell said, ignoring, perhaps tactfully, the little conflict between Nina and Mitch.

"Here we go again. Disagreement road." Mitch smiled at Nina and picked up their dialogue. "I told you I decided to go to the concert. I remember telling you."

"I don't remember," Nina said.

"Mitch," Lynell said, doing what, for her, was almost a coy pout, "you know I'm right about Escabardo. She was good, *but*—it's going out on a limb to call her impressive."

"Lynell, you know you're too critical."

"How can anyone be too critical, Mitch? If you have standards—"

"Standards, yes. Perfection, no, Lynell. Nobody's perfect. You have to give a little, make allowances . . ."

Nina, her head swinging from one to the other, said, "What is this, the traveling Lynell and Mitch Show?" They all laughed. A moment of good feeling. Nina handed Mitch his mail. Lynell put on her down vest.

"Well, I'd better be off," Lynell said. Then, to Nina, "Are you feeling all right?" She switched her long mane of hair over her shoulder. "You look a little pale."

"Cramps. They're making me feel really strange."

"Do you take anything?"

"I'm going to have some hot tea."

"Mmm, that's the best. Well, *ciao*. See you." She left.

Nina went into the kitchen and put water on to boil. "Who's your letter from?" she asked.

"Oh . . . my father."

He stood in the doorway, flapping the letter against his open palm.

"How come you're home so early?" Nina got down a tea bag and cup. "Want some tea?"

"No. Thanks."

"You're too full of pizza?"

He half smiled.

"Well?" she said.

"Well, what?"

"How come you're home now? Didn't you work today? *I* didn't, because the pipes in the office froze."

"Remember when I told you I might get laid off?"

he broke in. She nodded. "Well . . . it happened. I'm out of work."

"Oh, Mitch. Everything is happening today," she said sorrowfully. She leaned against the cupboard, her head buzzing with a distinct sensation of disaster— something bad was going to happen. She was going to flunk out . . . or, no, tomorrow there'd be a letter for her in the mail, saying her grandmother had died. Her heart pulsed in her throat. "What did they do, just tell you when you came in? No notice, nothing? Why are people so rotten!" She was nearly in tears.

"No, well . . ." He flapped the letter rapidly against his palm. "It didn't happen that way exactly." He sighed. "Actually, Nins, it was a couple of weeks ago."

"What do you mean, a couple of weeks ago? They laid you off a couple of weeks ago?"

"Right."

The tea kettle whistled. "Is this, is this some kind of joke, Mitch?"

"No."

"I don't get it. You've been laid off two weeks, and you never told me? I don't get it," she repeated.

He grimaced; a pained look turned down his mouth. "I should have told you . . . I don't know . . ." He bent his head, looking searchingly at the floor, as if down there he might find the answer to her question.

"I don't get it," Nina said for the third time.

"I kept hoping I'd find another job. . . . It's stupid, but I think what I wanted . . . I wanted to impress you with how fast I landed another job. Big fish. Then I didn't get a job, and I didn't get a job, and . . . it seemed like it got harder and harder to tell you. Like there just wasn't any right time to say, 'Hey, guess what happened to me. . . .' "

"You should have told me," she said, her throat filling. God, she was so emotional today. It was like being on a roller coaster.

"I know I should have. . . . I guess it was—vanity?"

"Is that why you've been so moody?"

"Mmmm. I guess that's it." He folded his arms. "I didn't know it would matter so much. I felt really put down by it. Like it was my fault. . . ."

"It wasn't, was it?"

"No. I told you, I was just low man on the totem pole. Somebody had to go. I was next in line."

"Then I still don't understand why you didn't say anything to me. It wouldn't have made any difference to me, Mitch. What'd you think I would do?"

"Nina, I'm trying to tell you, it wasn't logical. I don't pretend to understand everything about myself. All I know is I got really down on being out of work. I didn't want to talk about it! I felt"—he shrugged—"ashamed, I think. Anyway, every day I'd think, Today I'll find a job."

Nina poured the hot water, stirred the tea bag around, and added honey. "Tea?" she asked again. Mitch shook his head. "What'd you do all day?" Then she thought of something else. "You went out every morning, Mitch, just like you were going to work. Took a lunch and everything."

"I know. That was so you wouldn't guess. Mostly I looked for work. And I hung out in different places. Go to know the United States Employment Office very well. Sometimes, afternoons, I came home . . . then went out again before you came back so . . . you know, so you wouldn't catch on."

"You did that?" She sipped the tea. "Do you need money? I could lend you some."

"Thanks, that's nice, but I'm okay. I'm going to collect unemployment, and I had some bucks saved."

"Your car money?" He'd been planning to buy a car in the spring. He nodded. Nina's eyes fell on the pizza box. "Did Lynell know?"

"What?"

"That you were out of work."

She saw the answer in his face. "She knew! Mitch, that's . . . that's so . . ." Her eyes filled again. "That's so *bummy!*" She grabbed a napkin from the holder and blew her nose.

"What are you getting so upset about?" he said despairingly. "What difference does it make?"

"I'm the one who's living with you, Mitch!" She crumpled the napkin and threw it into the waste-basket. "How could you keep something like this from me and tell Lynell?"

"I was going to let you know as soon as I found work."

"Living together is supposed to mean sharing," she said in a choked voice.

Emmett stood up on his back legs, paws on the table. Nina swallowed, trying to clear her throat. "Hungry, baby?" She got a can of cat food from the cupboard.

"Are you feeding him again?" Mitch said. "Every time he opens his mouth—"

"Don't get started on that. Leave Emmett alone! You're always saying that. He doesn't have that much in his life. He has me, and he has food, and if he's hungry I'm going to feed him!"

"You're always making excuses for him, Nina. He's totally undisciplined. He doesn't even cover his shits. Lynell was practically holding her nose the whole time she was here."

"Maybe Lynell was holding her nose because the apartment stinks! And don't tell me it's Emmett's fault, because it isn't." This was crazy—fighting over Emmett. But she couldn't stop herself. The hell with being controlled. "You know, Mitch, it's a real foul mess in here, and now that I've found out you're not working, I'm wondering why I'm the one who usually does all the cleaning."

"What cleaning? You just said it was a foul mess."

"It is! And you know damn well it'll stay this way until I do something about it."

"Off my back, Nina. Off, off! I've had things on my mind."

"What things? Lynell?" Mitch stared at her. Lynell's name hovered between them like a poisonous insect. Appalled, Nina poured another cup of tea. The argument that had started out neatly to be about why Mitch hadn't told her he was out of work was spilling all over the place . . . like the hot tea which now sloshed over the edge of the cup, burning her hand.

"Damn," she whispered. She put her hand under the cold water.

"Did you say you had cramps?" Mitch said. "Your period? Is that why you're so—"

"I'm not so anything," she broke in. "Don't say that." She got her flannel nightgown. "I'm getting in bed."

"Listen, Nina." Mitch followed her into the other room. "You don't have to be so mad at me. I'm not trying to say I did right, but you're not utterly pure and righteous yourself."

"I don't keep things from you. I don't have secrets!"

"You sure of that? All that time you're alone with Leeman, or Seeman, or whatever his name is—"

"Lehman," Nina said. "Lehman. And I'm working when I'm with him."

"Right. Lay Man. Is he laying you, Nina?"

She pulled the nightgown over her head. Maybe if she stayed there in the friendly darkness of the nightgown tent and counted to ten slowly, all these nasty things they were saying to each other would disappear. "You want to take that back, Mitch?" she said as her head emerged.

"Should I?"

"You better, Mitch. You better!" She got into bed and pulled the covers up to her chin.

"Well, I'm not going to."

"Well, you should!"

"Well, too bad!"

They glared at each other like two bad ten-year-old kids. But by now Nina had lost track of why she was feeling so depressed. She only knew she hadn't come home that way. Was it the cramps? Lynell's knowing about Mitch's job? Mitch's nasty remark about Professor Lehman? *Her* nasty remark about Lynell? She couldn't sort it out. Everything had gotten all mixed up together. She didn't even want to think about it anymore. She was sick of the argument, sick of arguing. She wanted peace!

Mitch must have been sick of it, too, because he threw himself down next to her and said, "This is stupid."

"I agree."

"You want to make up?"

"Yes," Nina said.

They touched hands and a spurt of lust engulfed her. "Get in," she said. Mitch turned on the radio. The words of an old sixties song blared out. "She wore an itsy bitsy, teenie weenie, yellow polka dot bikini . . ."

"Shut that dumb song off," Nina said, but he never did.

Chapter
Twenty-two

Nicholas lived in an old two-family house with up-stairs and downstairs porches. The living room was filled with big comfortable-looking chairs, an old, red velvet couch and faded Oriental rugs thrown down helter-skelter on shining wooden floors. Nina looked around, surprised to see so much shabby furniture. She had expected Professor Lehman to live in a house where everything was new. Trailing after him, she caught cozy glimpses of an unmade bed, a frying pan on the stove, socks hanging over the shower bar. In the dining room the ceiling was bordered with strings of plaster roses.

"Here we are." He opened a door, put his hands on her shoulders, and propelled her into the room. There was a small desk, two chairs, a typewriter on a metal stand, and a small filing cabinet. An Oriental rug on the floor, and two windows looking out onto a yard.

"You didn't do all this since yesterday?" Nina said.

He laughed. "No, no, it's my home office. It's been this way forever." Nina sat down in front of the typewriter. "Ready to work already?" He laughed again.

"Yes," she said, smiling uncertainly. His mood had certainly improved since the day before.

"Well . . ." He fumbled around on the desk, then handed her one of the damaged yellow pads. "I thought you should try this first. Do you think you can make out any of it?"

She skimmed the page, then pointed to a paragraph in the middle. "That . . . that's readable . . ."

He looked over her shoulder, resting his chin lightly on her head. "Oh. Good. Yes, yes . . . you're right . . . Well, what you can't figure out, I'll either reconstruct from memory, or—"

"All that work. You did so much work, and just because of an accident. . . . It doesn't seem fair that it's all wiped out. . . ." She heard herself chattering; she was nervous, almost as jittery as when she first began working for him weeks ago and was so in awe of him she could hardly get out two sensible words in a row. But why now? Nervous, maybe, because she was in his house? It's an *office*, she told herself, a plain office, with a typewriter, stapler, pens and pencils. No different from his other office, where she had come to feel completely at ease.

"No," he was saying, "by this time in my life I know not to expect too much. Life rarely works out the way one wants it to." He leaned toward her, that same faint, amused, but warm smile on his face. "No use crying over things, Nina . . . no use at all. Life has too much to offer. . . ."

She was acutely aware of the smallness of the room, of heat rising and rising to her forehead, her ears, her lips.

"You'll see as you get older. One learns to stop banging one's head against walls. For instance, when I see something I want, I've learned to judge . . . is it possible? Can I have that? Or is that another stone wall? And I usually know. There are compensations in life." His eyes were luminous, shining the way they did at times when he lectured. He'd pull at his tie, roll up his sleeves, and his eyes would shine, shine with the excitement of his words.

I see something I want . . .

He means me. The thought jumped into Nina's mind. No, how ridiculous . . . conceited, actually. . . . Why would he be interested in her? The house, she thought distractedly, this place is overheated. Her hands were hot, swollen. "I should go to work." She heard her voice—high, peppy, artificial.

She rolled a sheet of paper into the typewriter. He sat down at the desk, a stack of papers in front of him. Gradually Nina became absorbed in reading the notes. The room was silent except for the clacking of the typewriter and the occasional faint rustle of pages turning.

"Break, Nina?"

She looked around. An hour had passed. She shook her hands from the wrist to take the tension out of her fingers.

Nicholas Lehman swiveled his chair toward her, put one hand firmly on each of her shoulders, smiled, and kissed her. This happened for Nina at the same slow, dreamlike pace that an accident might happen, so that she had time to know what was coming, while remaining frozen. Time to think, *He's going to kiss me . . .* and to see his face coming closer. . . . And then time to register her surprise, as his mouth met hers, that his lips tasted fruity, like oranges or plums.

All those daydreams . . . half dreams . . . those fantasies . . . *He's kissing me . . . Nicholas is kissing me. . . .* Like words to a song. . . . *Nicholas is kissing me. . . .*

And all the strength seemed to run out of her. . . . *Nicholas is kissing me. . . .* Her mind, her will, her will power was gone. Fled. She sat there being kissed. Waiting. She had abdicated: Nina, her *self,* the person who did or did not want, the one who said yes or no, that person was absent, lost in the daze of *Nicholas is kissing me.* A long kiss from which, finally, he withdrew his mouth and said, "Well . . . Well, that was certainly nice."

But she said nothing. Still sat there, dazed and waiting.

"Nina. You look so worried." He smoothed the line between her eyebrows.

"Oh . . . no . . . no . . ." Worried? Her? Worried about a kiss?

"I just wanted to kiss you," he said. "I didn't want to make you feel bad."

"Oh, no, no," she said again.

"Because we're friends. Aren't we friends?" He squeezed her hand.

"Oh . . . yes," she said this time. And began to come out of her daze. Friends? They were student and teacher. Employer and employee. Nicholas and Nina, older man, younger woman. Yes, all sorts of things. . . . But were they friends?

Calm down, she told herself. *Nothing happened. Just a kiss. A little kiss.*

"I like you," he said. "I like you very much."

He kissed me . . . Nicholas kissed me. . . .

"And . . . do you like me?" His eyebrows rose in charming, ironic question.

"Yes. . . ." Her head bobbed.

"So . . . you see . . ." He leaned toward her, kissed her again, this time on her nose. "Nothing to be afraid of!"

"No," she said, "I'm not afraid."

A few minutes later, saying something about needing to get home early, she left. *Just a kiss.* . . . Yes, just a kiss, she told herself again, walking away from his house. Some people thought no more of a kiss than a handshake or a squeeze on the shoulder. Sophisticated people kissed each other all the time. Darling! they said. Dearest! And then it was kiss, kiss, kiss.

Maybe he hadn't even intended it as a real kiss. It certainly wasn't the kind of kiss she and Mitch kissed sometimes, the kiss going on and on and on, drifting Nina into another world.

She straightened her back, hitched up her knapsack, and considered telling Mitch about the kiss. Just to prove how little it meant. How innocent it had been. A kiss between two friends.

Mitch, guess what?

What, Nins?

The funniest thing—I mean, funny-unexpected. Professor Lehman kissed me . . . just happened out of the blue. . . .

And then Mitch would say— Well, what would he say? *Nina, what the hell is going on? You let that guy kiss you?*

Crossing the street, Nina rearranged the scene. Begin from the beginning once more. *Mitch. Guess what? The funniest thing . . .*

And Mitch, calmly, *He kissed you? How was it?*

Nina, in a reflective way, *Ohhh, not bad. But not like your kisses.*

Well, Mitch would say reassuringly, *I hope you don't feel the least bit uncomfortable that he kissed you, Nins. Why, I've kissed someone recently, too.*

Really? Who's that? No, no, don't tell me. Let me guess. Sonia!

And Mitch, with a little chuckle, would nod and say, *You got it!*

Then, though she'd never before imagined Mitch that interested in Sonia, Nina became convinced she'd hit on something. All this time, foolishly, she had been nursing a little spark of jealousy about Lynell. Actually it was Sonia Mitch frankly admired. How many times had she heard him say complimentary things about Sonia? Many, many! She put the two of them together in her mind—Sonia so much shorter

than Mitch . . . her bracelets rattling . . . lips gleaming. . . .

But somehow it was easier to imagine Mitch and
Lynell. The two of *them* in the apartment. . . . In
the background that flute music Lynell liked so much.
. . . Certainly that made more sense than Sonia and
Mitch. It was Lynell that Mitch had told about losing
his job. Lynell who ate pizza with him and argued
about the pitch problems of that silly soprano! Yes,
Lynell and Mitch. *Lynell and Mitch.* Another ditty
she couldn't get out of her head. *Lynell and Mitch . . .
sitting in a tree . . . k-i-s-s-i-n-g.* . . . The words blotting
out what had happened in Nicholas Lehman's house.
Lynell and Mitch kissing . . . lying on the bed together. . . . Nina's skin prickled. She didn't like that
picture. Okay, maybe they kissed standing up, or
maybe she sat in his lap. And when they finished kissing, maybe they had one of their long yawn-making
discussions. Or did they talk about her? Laugh together when her name came up? Snicker because they
were kissing behind her back, and she was so incredibly naive she would never guess! Nina was breathing
with her mouth open, hot furious breaths.

So! Lynell and Mitch! Yes, she was in a fury, quite a
fury, a satisfying fury that occupied her whole mind.
It was only as she was going up the steps and thought
of facing Mitch that she came to her senses. Her face
turned violently hot. The image of Mitch and Lynell
faded. What remained was the memory of Nicholas
Lehman kissing her.

Chapter
Twenty-three

Over the weekend Nina dug out the notebook she sometimes wrote in. Privately she called it her journal. It had been lying untouched, for weeks, even months, in her drawer under a pile of socks and shirts. "I wish I could write down everything that has happened to me, everything I have thought and felt and experienced," she wrote. "Especially these last few weeks. I feel as if incredible amounts of time have passed, and as if I have grown and matured through experience. Things have happened to me I would not have thought possible, which maybe I dreamed about a little, but didn't think could actually come to pass." As soon as she wrote that, Nina became afraid to put down another word. What if Mitch discovered her journal?

Besides, side by side with a desire to write about Nicholas Lehman kissing her was another, equally strong impulse, and this was to blot out the whole episode. To erase it like a scrawled picture on a blackboard. Not to think about Nicholas Lehman. Not to remember the kiss. Not to wonder what it had meant or might mean to her in the coming days.

A cold rain fell all weekend and she and Mitch spent a lot of time indoors; but busy as she kept herself, it was impossible for Nina to perform that erasing trick. Just didn't work. If her mind was a blackboard, then there was the scrawled picture, complete in every detail.

Even when she wasn't consciously thinking about that Friday afternoon in Nicholas Lehman's house, even when she seemed fully occupied with showering or scrambling an egg or laughing with Mitch as they watched *Saturday Night Live,* there was still a hard tension, like a taut rope, in the back of her mind. A sense that the moment she let down her guard, the incident would come rushing back.

Then, too, in the most unexpected moments, grooming Emmett or looking idly out the window, or even going down the street to buy a box of corn flakes, a hot violent flush of feeling would come over her: an almost unbearable wave of sensuality mingled with vanity, pride, shame. He had kissed *her*! Could he not kiss any woman he chose? And then the shameful thought that she had sat there letting it happen, like a fourteen-year-old, numb and flattered. And what about her beliefs? What about fidelity? Honor? Trust? She and Mitch weren't married, true, but all the same, living together certainly meant *something*. She loved Mitch and she had been—well, not unfaithful, but not faithful, either!

Despite all this agitation she spent the weekend agreeably with Mitch, drinking wine, making love, and watching TV. Yet she also found herself monitoring their conversations and games, standing outside herself and commenting, as she had done at Christmas at home. One Nina romped and played, and another Nina carried on a not-to-be-quieted inner dialogue.

We're talking . . . lots of talk . . . maybe because I'm nervous? . . . True, but Mitch's talking, too, now that I know his "secret." . . . He's still very upset about being out of work. . . . I'd be upset, too, but in a different way. . . . Told him he must think it's a reflection on his masculinity. . . . He denied it—hotly! Said that was sidewalk psychology. . . . Putdown. Never know what to say when he comes out with stuff like that. . . . I thought he'd be interested, impressed maybe, that I figured that out. Made him mad, didn't it? . . . I should keep my mouth shut more. . . . He likes it when I listen. . . . So what? I like it when he listens, too!

Wonder if he talks to Lynell the way we talk? Both like classical music . . . big, intellectual discussions. . . . Boring, really; I wouldn't say that to either of them. . . . They say opposites attract. . . . Mitch and I sure are opposite. . . . Nicholas and . . . No, don't think about him. . . . I don't want to be upset. . . . We're having a good weekend . . . having fun . . . not even a little squabble over Emmett. . . .

They had a pillow fight, standing on the mattress,

batting wildly at each other, screaming like kids. "Gotcha!" "Ha, you missed!" "Dirty shot!" And even while she was laughing herself hoarse, that inner voice rattled on.

Hit him, but not too hard. . . . Watch it! . . . Oh, oh, no, it's okay. . . . Love his smile. . . . Professor Lehman's smile always makes me a little uncomfortable. . . . Don't know why, sort of think he's laughing at me. . . . Stupid thought? He's nice to me. . . . Oh, God. . . . Am I crazy? . . . I wish I could figure out that kiss. . . . Thought about it last night when Mitch and I . . . Made me feel guilty as hell. . . . Wonder if Mitch ever thinks about someone else when we're together. . . .

From Friday night to Sunday night, a half gallon of red wine disappeared. They were both in a bit of a wine glow all weekend. There was only one bad moment. This came when Mitch, standing in front of the mirror in his jockey shorts, said he could see where he'd put on weight since he lost his job. "I'm cutting out bread!"

"How about pizza?" Nina said before she could stop herself.

"That, too." A moment later he realized that had been a dig about Lynell, and he flushed. Nina fought the impulse to apologize. An uncalled-for remark, especially from her, but better not to call attention to it.

Monday morning was fresh and cool. Nina threw open the window, and at once Emmett was up on the sill, nose quivering like a pointer as he sniffed the air.

Nina and Mitch left the apartment together. "I

heard the candle works are hiring," he said. "I'm going there first."

"Good luck." Standing on the step above him, she shook his arm forcefully. "You're going to get a job. Maybe today. I feel it in my bones. You're going to get a job! Because I want you to."

He laughed up at her. "And so, because you want—"

"Yes!" She kissed him.

"You're nice to me," he said.

"Why shouldn't I be?"

The sun shone on the buildings. Pigeons flew up from the debris in the gutter. What a morning! Nina looked up to their window where Emmett sat on the sill. "Poor Em. He wants to get out so much."

"Nina . . ."

"Yes?" They moved slowly down the street holding hands. Mitch looked troubled. His hand was cold, almost clammy. Or was it hers? Today she had to go into Professor Lehman's classroom and look at him and listen to him, and already she knew that all she would be able to think about was Friday and the kiss.

She had come home in a blur that day and all weekend had worked at keeping herself under control and acting normal. Whereas Nicholas Lehman had probably forgotten the kiss two minutes later. She certainly didn't imagine that *he* had spent his weekend anguishing over it!

Then for the first time it occurred to her to wonder what he *had* thought of it. Had he liked kissing her? Had he done it truly in a friendly spirit? God, she wasn't that naive, was she? Well, then had he done it with evil intent, with seduction in his heart? She grimaced furiously. How she dramatized everything. Was there any doubt that the kiss had been an unimportant, even trivial, event to him?

"Nina," Mitch said again, then shook his head. "No . . . forget it." They parted at the corner, going in different directions.

"See you . . . see you later," she called after a few steps, turning to wave.

Mitch raised his hand over his head, but didn't look back. Nina's ears throbbed, and she was seized by the conviction that Mitch *knew*. Somehow, he knew about Friday. Was that what he'd been about to say? *I know what happened, Nina. You gave it away by the way you acted all weekend. God, you were so guilty! Guilt, guilt, guilt, was written all over your face! You let him kiss you, right? Right? Well, all I've got to say is, I'm really hurt and disappointed in you!*

She bumped into a girl carrying a huge leather portfolio under her arm. "Sorry . . . excuse me. . . ." Like a ship in a storm, she was quivering, listing from side to side. But what was the matter with her? Mitch didn't know. Just because he appeared a little subdued this morning—well, he still had job hunting on his mind.

Walking across campus, she told herself that ever since the kiss her perspective had been distorted. Worried about what Mitch knew—as if he had an inner line to her head. Talking to herself constantly. And now, half convinced she couldn't go to Nicholas Lehman's class. No, she decided, that would be cowardly.

But later, in his class, she sat with her head down

and never once looked directly at him. At the end of the session she left quickly with the other students and, feeling worn out by tension, decided she couldn't face going into work that day. She put in her time in the library. The next day, again, she fled to the library. How should she act when she was again alone with him? As if nothing had happened? Doubtful that she could carry that off. Would he mention the kiss? Or ignore it? Even if he acted the same as always, could she act natural with him? The problem was, even if she could, that would be what it was—acting. Maybe she should just quit the job. Great. And then Mitch would want to know why. And besides where was she going to find another job midway through second semester?

Back and forth she went, chewing on her ball-point pen, chewing over the situation till her teeth ached. Looking at the other students sitting in the carels and at the long tables, heads bent over books, she wondered if anyone else worried the way she did. What was this huge fuss about? What had this earthshaking event been? A kiss. Two mouths meeting for ten seconds. And she'd been agonizing over it for days! Why did she take everything so seriously? Too seriously! All she had to do was show up the next day as usual, sit down in front of the typewriter, take one of the long yellow legal pads—and type. Say nothing, show nothing, do nothing but what she had been hired for!

It was still sunny when she left the library. The streets were thronged with couples, joggers, Frisbee players, dog walkers, and bikers. Nina walked home slowly, and basking in the relief of finally having made a decision (and one that seemed sensible to her), she was able to enjoy the air. Maybe it really was spring!

Across the street from their building, music poured out of loudspeakers fastened to the facade of the record shop. "Show me how you feel . . . don't hide behind your eyes. . . ." Nice! "Show me how you feel," she sang under her breath, "don't hide behind your eyes. . . ." She wanted to remember that. There was something special about music that summed up an idea or an emotion. Maybe she ought to write that down in her journal.

Going up the stairs, she met Mitch coming down. "Hi!" she said. "Coming out to meet me?"

"What?"

"Were you coming out to meet me?" she repeated. There was a strange expression on his face, a wounded, tentative smile. "What happened?" she said. "Did something happen?"

"Nina . . ." He put his hand on her arm, blinked. "Listen, don't worry." He squeezed her arm. "Emmett got out. He got away, but—"

Nina heard him, but the words didn't register for a minute. She was still in the glow that had come with having settled something in her mind and then, relieved, walking home, almost prancing, sniffing the new spring air. Like Emmett. Oh, how he had sniffed at the opened window this morning! His whole body had lengthened like an arrow seeking the target. Air! Spring! The world! And then he had looked up at her pleadingly. Clearly he'd been saying, Let me out, won't you let me out for just a little while? And she had petted him, spoken to him soothingly. "I'm sorry, baby, you just can't . . . you're too old . . . not a street cat anymore."

She looked at Mitch. "He got out?" she said. "Emmett?" Mitch nodded miserably. And for one baffled moment, she thought, *Because of the kiss.* . . . As if Emmett's breaking free was her punishment. Then her head cleared. Energy poured through her like a jet of boiling steam. "Emmett got out? You let Emmett get *out,* Mitch?" She ran back down the stairs, Mitch close behind her.

Chapter
Twenty-four

Their feet clattered on the steps. "I was just going out to look for Emmett again," Mitch said.

"What do you mean—again?"

"He got out . . . a couple hours ago. I went after him, but—"

"A couple hours ago?" Nina's voice rose.

"I looked for him, Nina. Lynell and I—"

"Lynell?"

"She came up to the apartment . . . that's when he got out. . . ."

Nina raced around the turn. *Lynell*. Damn. What did it mean? Emmett out! Who had been so careless? Lynell?

"When I opened the door for her—you know Emmett—he went out like a streak of lightning."

"Why didn't you stop him?" Her knapsack thumped on her back.

"Tried to. I didn't think that fat old guy had it in him, Nina." Mitch's voice brightened. "He went down those stairs so fast! You should have seen him. It was amazing."

"How about the front door? How'd he get out the front door?"

"We should have caught him there," Mitch said, "but some idiot had left it wide open."

Nina ran outside. The same record was playing. The same chorus. *Show me how you feel . . . don't hide behind your eyes. . . .*

"Where'd you look for him?"

"All around, checked out the alleys, everything."

"Where? Where exactly?" She glanced up and down the crowded street. "Which way? Which way did you go?" Without waiting for an answer she started off, walking fast, eyes down, checking out the street, across the street, glancing into doorways and behind cars, looking for the familiar broad face and striped tail. Emmett was old and slow—yes, fat, too, Lynell and Mitch had been right about that—and half blind, as well. How would he ever defend himself against other cats? What if a dog got him? There were always dogs roaming the neighborhood, sniffing garbage pails, their lips pulled back in savage grins.

Mitch was behind her. "Go the other way," she said. "Go look somewhere else!"

Mitch turned off at the corner. Nina half walked, half ran. *Emmett . . . come on, Emmett, where are you? Stupid cat! You had your fun. . . . Come on, it's*

getting late. . . . *I've got a can of tuna fish for you* . . .
real tuna fish, not that tuna-fish-flavored junk. . . .

A cat meowed. Nina looked around. A tiny, all-
black cat rolled on its back on the sidewalk, then got
up and rubbed against her leg. Emmett wouldn't get
lost, would he? What of all those stories about cats
finding their way home after being set down hundreds
of miles away? Or was that only dogs? She imagined
Emmett trotting patiently along the side of the inter-
state, on his way home to Hawley, thousands of cars
and huge freight trucks whizzing by. . . . And what
would he eat? Hunt for his food? It had been years
since he'd hunted, and even then he'd never had to
hunt seriously. Well-fed, he'd catch a mouse, a bird, a
chipmunk, play with it, bat it into the air, and finally
deposit the limp body, sometimes headless, on their
doorstep. A little gift she didn't want. "It's your cat,"
her mother would' say. "You get rid of that chipmunk." And Nina would have to pick up the stiff,
bloody little corpse and throw it in the garbage.

At those times she had come as close as she ever did
to disliking Emmett. "It's just nature," Nancy said.
"He doesn't know what he's doing. Doesn't know he's
killing any more than he knows he loves you." Nina
had believed the part about killing, but not about
loving. She didn't care what anyone said. Emmett
loved her. He knew her voice, knew her habits, had
comforted her at times when she was depressed. More
than once he'd licked her tears from her face. And
right now, if he was lost or confused or hurt, he'd be
waiting for her to find him and make things right.

She walked by him without seeing him. He was in

the gutter on Cooper Avenue. She saw him out of the corner of her eye. A cat sprawled in the gutter, one leg turned crookedly. She walked past him. One step, two steps. Then turned and went back. He must have been hit by a car. There was dried blood around his nose. Bending to pick him up, Nina moaned.

In the apartment she put Emmett on the table first, then a moment later laid him carefully down on the bed. She smoothed his fur, tried to arrange his head so he looked like he was sleeping. Where was Mitch? She wanted to tell someone who'd known Emmett that he was dead.

She went to the window, tapped restlessly on the pane, then picked up the phone and dialed her old number. Busy. She dialed again immediately. On the fourth ring Sonia answered. "Look, D.G. I mean it!"

"It's me," Nina broke. "Nina."

"Oh, Nina. I was so sure it was going to be D.G. We're having a little fight."

"Is Lynell there? I want to tell her something. Wait, no, I'll tell you first. Emmett's dead."

"Emmett?" Sonia said disbelievingly.

"He got out. He was hit by a car."

"Oh, poor Emmett." Sonia started crying. "Nina, you must be feeling terrible. Do you want me to come over? I'm coming over, Nina."

"All right." In fact, at the moment she was calm, yet full of a restless energy. As she hung up the phone Mitch came in.

"I couldn't find him."

"I found him," Nina said.

"You did! Great! That's just great," he said. "Where was he?"

Nina pointed to the bed and watched closely as Mitch bent toward Emmett, then jerked back. "What is—he's hurt," he said, sounding confused.

"He's dead," she said. "He got hit by a car. I knew he'd get hit by a car if he went out. That's what I always said, didn't I, Mitch?"

"God, Nina, I'm sorry!" He sat down abruptly. "You must feel terrible." Sonia's exact words.

"I don't feel good." She picked up Emmett and walked around the room with him.

Mitch put his arms around her. "I'm sorry, Nins. I'm really sorry."

"Okay." She shrugged off his arms. Just wanted to be alone with Emmett. She paced the room, cradling him like a baby. He was heavy.

Mitch put music on the stereo. Nice, soft music. Funeral music, Nina thought. Her nose stiffened. Her whole face was stiff and masklike. She kept walking up and down, back and forth, not pausing, sometimes shifting Emmett's weight a little, but continuously moving; just had to keep moving.

"Aren't you going to sit down?" Mitch asked after a while.

"No."

"Nina, you can't just—"

"Sonia's coming over," she said intensely. "I tried to get Lynell, but she wasn't in. Sonia cried."

"Nina." Mitch took her by the shoulders. "Take it easy. Come on, sit down, relax." She just looked at

him until he dropped his hands. "You want something to eat?" he asked. "How about a glass of milk?"

"No."

"I'll make you a sandwich, a tuna fish sandwich—"

"*No.*"

He read for a while, then put down his book.
"Nina, what are you going to do with it?"

"Do?"

"With the"—he gestured—"him. What are you
going to do with him?"

"Sonia's coming over," she said again in a stubborn
voice.

"Nina, you've been walking around with it for an
hour already."

"Not *it,* Mitch. Emmett." She looked at him hard.
She wasn't saying anything. She wasn't accusing him
of killing Emmett. She knew he was sorry, but . . . he'd
been careless. He knew Emmett! Knew how he was
always trying to get out. *Criminally* careless.

"I'll take care of Emmett for you," Mitch said. "I'll
do it. You don't have to think about it."

"Take care of him?"

"We can put him in the— He's got to be buried. I'll
do it, Nins."

"*No.*" She held Emmett tighter.

"Nina, listen, you can't just—"

A knock on the door, and Sonia came in. She put
her arms around Nina. Nina didn't say anything, just
waited until Sonia released her, then started pacing
again.

"Don't you want to sit down?" Sonia said. Why was
everyone saying the same things to her? She held Em-

mett close to her face. He was getting stiff. She wondered if he had enjoyed his adventure. Did he die happy? Or had he just been confused and frightened out on the street? Stupid of her! How could he die happy being smashed by a car?

"I'm going to make some food," Mitch said. "I think you should eat, Nina."

"I'm not hungry."

"Make her something anyway," Sonia said. She went into the kitchen with Mitch, saying she'd left a note for Lynell and she'd also called D.G., who was coming over in a little while.

"Lynell knows about Emmett already, Sonia," Nina said in a loud voice.

Sonia looked out the kitchen door. "She knows?"

"She was here when Emmett got out," Nina said in the same loud voice. "That's how it happened, Sonia. She came up here, Mitch opened the door, and Emmett got out. They didn't catch him. Neither of them could catch him, Sonia."

"Nina, Nina," Mitch said. "You make it sound like we let him go on purpose. I told you we chased him all the way out to the street. I told you we looked everywhere for him."

"Oh, I know, I know. You looked everywhere for him. They looked everywhere for him, Sonia. Mitch was just going to look for him again when I came home. Right, Mitch?"

"Come on, Nina," he said, coming into the room. "Hang on there; you're going over the edge."

"Oh, I am not," she said, but she sat down suddenly with Emmett in her lap. "Don't be ridiculous. Don't be such a turd, Mitch." She had the childishly satisfying thought that right now she could say anything she wanted to Mitch, and he wouldn't dare answer back. She stroked Emmett's fur, trying to get it to lie down nicely. It was stiff and greasy, not like his fur at all.

Mitch and Sonia sat down at the table and ate scrambled eggs. "Nina," Sonia said, "we made the eggs with cheese. They're really good. Come on over and eat some."

"I'm not hungry, and I don't see how you can eat. I think it's pretty coldhearted of both of you." But secretly she thought that she was the coldhearted one. She hadn't shed a tear. A couple times she had thought she was going to cry, but then she didn't. Was something wrong with her? Years ago, in his heyday, Emmett would often come limping home from fights with other cats, and over those little scratches she had cried buckets. Now—nothing.

While Sonia and Mitch were still eating, Lynell and D.G. came in on each other's heels. Lynell looked at the cat, shaking her head and pushing her hair behind her ears with a nervous gesture. "Boy, tough luck, Nina, " D.G. said in a sorrowful voice. "Anyway, he was old. I mean, that doesn't make it any better, but you know what I mean. I guess he didn't have that many years left anyhow." D.G. sat down at the table to eat the eggs Nina didn't want.

"Tell Nina she has to get rid—she has to bury him, or something," Mitch said.

Who was he talking to? Lynell? No. He'd hardly looked at her. One glance when she came in, then he acted like she wasn't even there. Did he think Nina didn't notice? She wasn't blind and deaf just because Emmett was dead. Guilty—that was it. Mitch felt guilty and so did Lynell. Because they had been stupid and careless and thoughtless and rotten! Neither of them had liked Emmett. Mitch had pretended, but she knew better. What about all those jokes he and Lynell were always making about Emmett? Saying wouldn't he make a lovely cat scarf. And how he was a walking argument for euthanasia. Her stomach churned.

"Nina, Mitch is right," Sonia said. "I know how you feel, hon. I know how I'd feel if Heidi died, but you've got to do something about him. Can't just keep him that way. You know."

"Okay, okay." They were all talking to her as if she were two years old. Why had they even come? She'd never seen Lynell look so uncomfortable. How hard had she looked for Emmett? Nina could imagine her, standing on one leg, saying offhandedly, "Oh, that fat pig'll come home when he gets hungry."

"Who wants ice cream?" Mitch said.

"What kind?" D.G. asked.

"Chocolate chip. Or did we buy mocha chip this time, Nina?"

"Go home!" she said. What was this, a party? They all looked at her, then away.

"Well, maybe we ought to go," D.G. said, but he filled a bowl with ice cream.

Finally they left. As soon as they were gone Nina went to the door with Emmett. "Where're you going?" Mitch said. "What're you going to do?"

"Find some place for him. Bury him," she said flatly. "He's dead; he's got to be buried."

"Nina, why don't you let me take care—"

"I don't want Emmett in a garbage can!"

"Okay, don't get upset. I'll come with you."

Outside, Nina walked toward a street where the college was pulling down old houses, and nothing but empty lots remained. An empty lot didn't seem too bad a place to bury Emmett. He'd probably had lots of good times in empty lots.

It was nearly dark; the rim of the sky was greenish. Nina wandered around holding Emmett in her arms. She hadn't brought anything to dig with. "Nina," Mitch said, "let's go back, this is crazy. You can't bury him here. The ground is still frozen. Even if you had a shovel— Look, Nina, I know how you feel."

She picked up a rock, and holding Emmett in one arm, began scraping at the ground. Mitch sighed and knelt down next to her. "At least put him down." He picked up a rock and worked with her, loosening the soil. Sweat broke out on Nina's forehead. Neither of them said anything. There were only the sounds of cars passing and the stones scraping at the earth.

Mitch sat back on his heels. "We're not going to be able to dig a grave, Nina."

"I'm not going to just leave him here, Mitch!"

"I didn't say you should."

"And I won't burn him, either. Or put him in the garbage!" She smiled furiously and laid Emmett in the shallow depression they'd made. She began piling stones around him.

"You'll have to cover him, too," Mitch said.

Hunkered down, her face closed like a fist, Nina continued making a stone mound around Emmett's body.

"I really think you have to cover him, too, Nina."

"I'll do it." Her voice was thin as the last finger of sunlight lying across the treetops. She put the first rock on Emmett, felt his body sinking beneath the weight like a pillow. She took a rock Mitch handed her and set it down next to the first one. "More."

Emmett was covered. Nothing to be seen but a hump of rocks and stone. She wanted to say a prayer for him, but nothing came.

Chapter Twenty-five

On the way home after burying Emmett, Nina said, "I don't blame you, Mitch, I know you didn't mean to let him out." Worn out by emotion, she staggered like a drunk. Mitch took her arm and held it close to him.

In the morning she woke up feeling blank and depressed. The day passed slowly. She went from class to class, catching a handful of words here, a sentence there. In Nicholas Lehman's classroom, she sat with her notebook open, pen in hand. But she heard almost nothing. Why had she told Mitch she didn't blame him? Why so quick to say that?

A LIE, she wrote in her notebook. She put little lines around the words so they shone like stars. A LIE. A shining lie. Yes, she blamed him. She *blamed* him. Who else? Emmett? He wasn't responsible for his own

death. He had only known the moment. And Mitch—
had he only known the moment, too? Talking to Lynell, he had left the door open. What had they been
saying that was so important? So utterly absorbing
that Mitch had forgotten how Emmett always, always,
always made his try for freedom?

Was she being unfair? Could it have happened anytime, to anyone? To her, too? What about that time
Mitch and she were fighting and Emmett had run out
into the hall? Yes, but even with her head throbbing,
she'd gone after him. She'd called him in a voice he
couldn't ignore and brought him back inside.

At the end of the class period she moved toward the
door. "Miss Bloom." Nicholas Lehman perched on the
edge of his desk, a pencil between his fingers. "Will
you be able to do some typing today?"

Why not? What else did she have to do? If she
didn't work, she had to go home. She'd gone home
yesterday. Gone home and met Mitch on the stairs. . . .
Mitch would be home today, too. She would have to
talk to him. Maybe even smile to show she didn't
blame him . . . to keep the shining lie alive. Smile,
smile very hard because otherwise she might say, *You
killed my cat. You killed Emmett.* She had to remember that he had, in a moment of carelessness, only left
the door open. Left it open just a second too long.
Easy to do! He hadn't put a rope around Emmett's
neck. He hadn't fed Emmett poisoned meat or taken a
gun and shot him like an old horse. And, what's more,
Mitch had been sincerely sorry, nearly abject. How
mean and unfeeling it would be of her to jump on
Mitch when he was miserable enough already. First no

job, now his fault that Emmett was dead. Why rub it in? Why pound on him? But she kept fantasizing running at him with both fists curled, screaming *You killed my cat! Cat killer!*

Oh, yes, how satisfying that would be. Did she really have to be so restrained? Why was she worrying about his feelings? The hell with his feelings! She was going to go home and tell him, give it to him straight, and if she made him cry, all the better. Let him cry enough tears for her, too!

"Nina—?" The room had emptied. Nicholas Lehman smiled slightly. "Wool gathering?"

"Pardon me?" Dizzy, she held on to the edge of his desk.

"I, ah, wondered if you'd be able to type today?"

She stared at him. Would he care that her cat was dead? She realized she was not being entirely lucid. She was definitely not thinking straight, was probably even a little crazy today. She had to be careful. Careful not to say things she'd be sorry for, sorry for later on. Was Mitch still sorry, sorry? Or had he forgotten already? Used up all his sorries yesterday? *I'm sorry, Nina . . . I'm sorry, Nina. . . .* He must have said that six times. At least.

"I'll type. Yes, I'll be in to type today." Her neck quivered; there was a quivering little smile on her face.

"Terrific." Nicholas Lehman tossed her a key. "Let yourself into the house. I'll see you there."

Sparrows squabbled in the trees. The apartment was quiet. Nina put in a sheet of paper, typed words, typed sentences, filled the page. She put in another sheet. Her fingers hung on the keys. "Oh, what for?" she said. "What for?" She put her head down and cried at last. Cried and cried and cried. Stupid to grieve so over a cat, but it was Emmett. . . .

"Nina. Nina!" She hadn't heard him come in. He put his hand on her head, knelt down next to her. "What's the matter? Can I help?" His eyes were on a level with hers. Would he have wanted to put Emmett into the garbage?

"Oh . . . please . . ." she said. Didn't know why she said it. What she meant or wanted. "Oh, please . . ."

"Your hands are like ice." He warmed them between his, and she moved toward him, seeking blindly for comfort. That was what she wanted—comfort. *Hold me, comfort me. . . . Please comfort me.* He was holding her. Couldn't he hold her tighter? She burrowed into him, to be close, to be close and comforted. They were falling down on the rug, falling, falling, falling . . . close, close, close . . . She heard someone crying, little mewing sounds, oh, oh, oh, it was her. . . . And all this was mixed with her tears.

Chapter
Twenty-six

"God, I hope I land this job," Mitch said fervently. "Pray for me, Nina." He had just walked in with the news of a lead on a job driving a delivery truck for Ferry's, an office supply firm. "The guy seemed to like me, but you never know. . . . Keep your fingers crossed! Don't walk under any ladders!" He laughed. "Do you know what I realized today? It's totally demoralizing to be out of work. I've actually been a little crazy. Absolutely a little deranged. Depressed? Hell, yes. Just not myself, not looking at the world with a very healthy attitude. I didn't realize how bad I'd been until the boss at this place—Ferry's—until he said 'Well, come on back Monday and we'll talk.' He said, 'I've got one or two more guys to see.' I said, 'Okay, fine, but my chances are good?' He said, 'Sure. Good as the next one.' Then he winked. 'Maybe better,' he said. I tell you, Nina, those two words and that wink, and I walked out of there on air. Ten feet high! I felt so *good*. That's when I realized—I've been on the ropes for weeks! I really forgot what it feels like to feel good. Do you know what I mean? Am I making sense?'' he asked exuberantly.

"Sure. Sure you are. And . . . and I'm really happy for you," Nina added after a moment. Wasn't that what was expected? The normal, ordinary, confident, I-believe-in-you sort of remark a loving girl friend would make to her boyfriend? She looked at Mitch to see if she had struck the right note. He was smiling, so it must be okay. It seemed to her that for the present, anyway, she had lost some vital connection: a link between hearing and speech that told her—and told her quickly—what was a correct response.

"That's wonderful, Mitch." She poured energy into her voice. "I'm not at all surprised. Why shouldn't they hire you?" She gave his hand a squeeze for good measure.

For the last few days she had cut Nicholas Lehman's classes. If figuring out how to act after he kissed her had given her trouble before, understanding what was required of her *now* was close to disastrous. She simply didn't know how to handle this situation. Once again she was spending her afternoons in the library, study- ing, or appearing to. Her concentration was ragged. A few sentences read, a few notes taken, and the fidgets overtook her. She would scrape her chair around, shove papers together, and sharpen pencils with her old elementary school plastic sharpener. It was a small, clear pink device made in the shape of a pig. You stuck the pencil in the pig's snout. Pencil sharpening absorbed her. So did lining up the edges of the tabs in her notebook. But eventually she would remember. Emmett was dead, and she had made love with Professor Lehman.

There was an equation there, somehow. The two extraordinary events were linked, but for moments at a time the link escaped her. Her mind was clouded. Then—oh, yes!—she understood. Because of Emmett's death, she had been in need. A needy person. A person who needed comfort. But not Mitch's comfort.

Leaving Nicholas Lehman's house that afternoon, she had squinted painfully at the light glaring off the sidewalk. Still early in the afternoon. She hadn't been in his house very long at all. But long enough. . . . A girl from one of her classes had jogged by, ponytail flapping. "Hi, Nina!" Why did joggers always look either smugly happy or excruciatingly miserable? Was there no in-between anywhere? Why had she worried so over a kiss? Worried immoderately over what she now saw as a sweet and innocent meeting of mouths? She longed for that moment again, when all she had committed was an error in judgment. All she had done was make a little mistake. A mistake—such a soothing word: clearly something that could be put right. A misstep. A missed step? No. A wrong step. A step off the path. Serious, but not fatal. Whereas what she had done in Nicholas Lehman's office was more like a plunge over a cliff. Once that step off the cliff had been taken, there was no crying *Wait! I've changed my mind! I didn't mean that!*

"Don't let me oversleep Monday morning," Mitch said. "That's when I go in to see that guy again."

"No, I won't."

"Eh! I'll probably be up at the crack of dawn anyway."

"Probably."

"You know what, Nina? Something else I realized today. I miss old Emmett. I got used to him, and I really miss him."

She didn't answer.

"I noticed it tonight, coming home. Miss the old cat. To my surprise! If I could change that day, Nina . . ." Hands in his back pockets, he walked restlessly around the room. "I'd do it over from top to bottom. You know that, don't you? Emmett being killed—it's like it's all part of that bad time. Besides everything else, I know I haven't been the easiest person to live with."

"No . . . no . . ."

"Oh, come on, don't deny it. I know, I know what I've been like."

"No, it wasn't that . . . It was all right . . . and . . ." Her voice trailed off. With every word she wondered that Mitch didn't see her agitation, wondered that she didn't give herself away, give away what had happened on the worn Oriental rug in Nicholas Lehman's office.

"At least I caught up on my movies," he said, sitting down in the old chair. "I got so sick of hitting the hiring offices, hearing them say no. No, no, no! No applications, no jobs, no hiring. No, we don't want you!"

"Movies?" The conversation had taken an odd turn.

"I saw dozens," Mitch confirmed. "I'd just flake out on job hunting after a while and drop into a movie and sit there all afternoon. I saw *Raiders of the Lost Ark* four times. . . . Come here, sit next to me." He patted the broad seat of the old velvet chair.

"Sounds like you had fun, at least," Nina said brightly. She brushed at the seat. Cat hairs. "You didn't tell me that about the movies before."

"I guess not. I just didn't want to admit . . . Here you were, going to school, studying, working, putting in your time, and me— What was *I* doing? I didn't tell you a bunch of stuff," he added. "Can you guess?"

"Guess?"

"You know," he said. "I have a feeling you know."

Nina's heart beat very hard, as if what he was saying was *I* know. *I know all about you and Nicholas Lehman.* Then such a complicated mixture of emotions shook her—she began to tremble, as if a giant hand had her by the scruff of the neck—that she found it impossible to continue the conversation. "Let's not hang around here tonight," she cried, jumping up. "I want to do something that's fun. I want to eat out. I want to eat Chinese food. Winter Melon Soup."

"Winter Melon Soup in spring?"

"Yes, why not? Don't you want to eat Winter Melon Soup?" She laughed vivaciously and ran to the closet. "Come on, Mitch, come on, let's get dressed up, let's go out and eat. Let's be happy!"

Chapter
Twenty-seven

On Monday Nina went to Nicholas Lehman's class. She had to go back sometime. Today Mitch would find out if he had a job. Today she would find out . . . what? She opened her notebook, took out her pen, and waited. The lecture was on Hemingway. "What do we know about Ernest Hemingway? A great deal on the surface. He lived his life as if it were a novel." Nicholas Lehman was wearing a checked sport shirt, a tie loosely knotted under the collar. One leg up on a chair, he jabbed his finger to make a point. "Writing was agony for Hemingway. If he could write two, three hundred words a day—good words, as he said—he was satisfied."

Nina had never seen Nicholas Lehman look so attractive, so vivid. She stared, looked away. Had she really . . . ? Yes, and with him. . . . What would freckled Kim, sitting next to her, think if she knew? Oh, but that was vanity, and not pretty vanity. Nina winced for herself. The point was she had avoided him for several days, but resolved nothing. Or perhaps there was nothing to resolve? Perhaps this storm in her head was also vanity?

He stopped her as she left the room. "Miss Bloom. Could you stay for a minute?"

She stood at the corner of his desk, knapsack slung over one shoulder. People streamed past, glancing at her. Did anyone guess? Did something show on her face? Nicholas smiled good-bye to two girls who smiled brilliantly, longingly, back. Was that how she had smiled at him in the beginning?

She focused on a tiny hole in his jacket near the fourth button. The same elbow-patched tweed he'd worn all year. The last student left. He looked at her, said nothing. She stood there, her head slightly bowed, a kind of fatalism, dry and tough as a cactus, settling in her heart. She was worn out by emotion, by the effort of trying to weigh and balance and understand, by the seemingly impossible chore of putting events in order. She wanted things not to be haphazard; to *mean,* to signify. . . . But all weekend she had been thinking, What if everything that happened had all been worked out beforehand? What if she had had no choices? What if right now, for instance, she was only playing out her part?

She waited for him to speak. She was tired, too tired. Let him speak first. But what would she say if he were to ask her, point blank, *Well, Nina, what about*

us? How would she answer? *We . . . I . . . it was . . .
something happened. . . . Let's not . . .* Her thoughts
ran into each other. She stared at him, wishing he
were less attractive, wishing she remembered less of
that afternoon.

And now, what was this look he was giving her? A
long straight look, a warm smile, and then a nod, a
wry set of his mouth as if he were coming to some not-
too-surprising conclusion. But finally he only said,
"You weren't in class last week."

"No. Well . . . I was studying, in the—in the library."

"I believe those are the first cuts you've taken all
year?"

"No. I took one other."

"Ah, that's right. Recently, too. Studying then, also,
hmm? And here I thought you didn't want to see me."
Then that engaging smile. He glanced toward the
open door. His hand went to his tie, and he straightened it. But still that smile. Was he laughing at her?
Did he think she was just a dumb little sophomore,
that he could—

Flushing, she rose up on her toes. *Look, I admit
I'm naive, but I'm not totally dumb. You can't just . . .
you can't push me around! I won't let you.* She was
making a speech. It roared through her. She forgot
how tired she was. *Look, it happened, but it didn't
mean anything. I've given it lots of thought. It was
a—a—an accident! I needed something, and you were
there, and it happened. I don't want to attach any
importance to it. It happened. It shouldn't have, but
it did. And now let's not ever mention it again!*

He leaned against the desk. "I want to ask you something." The windows were open, the faded green shades flapping in the breeze. "What do you think of me?"

"What do I—? I think—" Oh, Nina! Speak up! Tell him about how it just happened; how you've thought about it, and you should both let it drop now. Give him that wonderful speech. "You're . . . well, very nice, and—and good to work for," she prattled like an eight-year-old.

He put up his hand, wincing, smiling. "I didn't want a personality rating. Let me put it another way. To be blunt about it, do you feel I forced the situation? I'm referring, of course, to, ah, ah—do you think I, ah, put pressure on you the other day?"

Was he nervous? Was that possible? Surely not more nervous than she! As if to prove it, she gave an abrupt, strained laugh.

"I want you to be honest with me," he said. "The whole ah, ah, episode was very delightful, but I wouldn't want to think that I—"

"No," she said, "it happened because—"

"I wanted it to happen," he said. "Did you know that?" He smiled again, but differently; the tinge of self-deprecation had vanished. "Did you know I wanted to make love to you?"

She could only shake her head. Had it all happened, then, because *he* had made it happen? And where was she in that scene? Where was her grief, her want, her need? Her guilt?

"Surely you knew. Come on, now, you girls today are smart, smarter than that. You knew. Yes? And you were thinking about it for a long time. . . . As long as I was. Put down that knapsack, will you? You look like you're ready to take off at any moment."

She gripped the sack more tightly. It seemed the one thing anchoring her solidly to the ground, to herself. Her thoughts flew in every direction. What did he want? What was he saying? About himself? About her?

"It wasn't your fault," she said. She wanted to explain it all to him, make him understand. She hadn't just been standing there like one of those big rubber toys waiting to be knocked over.

"Fault? Fault?" he said impatiently. "Where does that word come in? I didn't think that was in your generation's vocabulary. What I was asking, what I was interested in knowing. . . . When we made love, it was voluntary?"

Voluntary? She nodded uncertainly. Nina Bloom, volunteer army of one. No conscription. No draft. No draft dodging, either. And no dodging what he was leading up to now, leaning in closer to her, one hand warmly on her shoulder.

"So then . . . I'd like to see you again. You can continue working, your typing. . . . We won't change that. And we'll, ah, ah, work the other out." He straightened the collar of her shirt, kissed her. Her legs were languid with heat, and she felt an impulse to lean back . . . to let happen what would happen. . . . Later on she'd say, Well, it happened, just happened. . . .

He crossed to the door, shut it quietly. He pulled a shade, touched the shade to quiet it. The room was dim, and he kissed her again.

His hand tangled in her hair, tugged her toward him. Nina's stomach jerked. She seemed to come awake. His hand in her hair . . . pulling her toward him. And he was smiling, smiling. "Don't," she said. Tried to twist her lips into a sophisticated smile . . . to say something dazzling and final. "You're hurting me," came out in a whine-howl. And then again, stronger, "Don't!"

"What is it? What—?"

"My hair. My _hair,_" she said, with the utmost seriousness, as if this word contained all her anger, her panic, her doubt and certainty. She took his hand, freed her hair. They stared seriously at each other. And his lips drew back: a smile like a dog whose bone has been taken away.

"No," she said. "No, I can't. I can't do . . . that. Again. I won't." And she ran. The door banged behind her. Down the empty corridor she ran, her footsteps clattering. God, oh, God, had she said it; had she done it? Humiliated, relieved, she ran all the way home, shaking with reckless laughter.

Chapter
Twenty-eight

"Hi, adorable." A girl sitting on a roof yoo-hooed to Mitch. "You're taken, huh?" She wriggled her toes.

Mitch saluted her. "Sorry."

In shorts and sandals, Nina and Mitch moved slowly through the masses of students who had come out to worship the sun. Orange Frisbees whirled through the air. Earthworks, a brass band, played on the concrete apron outside the library, the band members, in jeans and torn T-shirts, booming out their challenge to the raucous shouts shooting out of every open window. It was a Saturday in late April, but hot as a day in July. The bare trees shimmered in the heat while beneath them forsythia and magnolia were in shining bloom.

Eating ice-cream cones, Nina and Mitch gawked

like a pair of tourists. They passed a couple, both in bikinis, both gleaming with grease, lying side by side, holding metal shields up before their faces with the rapt, intense look of artists. The roofs of every building, the balconies, the steps and lawns, were packed with couples.

Mitch threw away the bottom of his cone. "You look cute, did I tell you?"

Her hair was in braids, she'd put on dangly earrings and a plaid cap. "You look cute, too." He was wearing his FERRY'S, THE BIGGEST CLIP JOINT IN TOWN T-shirt and a baseball cap.

"You know what I've been thinking? We should get another cat."

"I really don't want—" she began, then ahead she saw Nicholas Lehman, in jeans and sunglasses, coming out of the library.

"We could get a breed," Mitch said. "An Abyssinian, or a Siamese."

"No," Nina said. "Not yet." Professor Lehman walked toward them.

"Siamese are exceptionally smart animals. And beautiful. They have blue eyes."

And now Nicholas Lehman had seen her, too. "Miss Bloom," he said coolly.

"Hello, Professor Lehman." Astonishing how calm she sounded. Astonishing how much she did not want to meet him this way, with Mitch. Two weeks had passed. He never looked at her in class, never spoke to her. She had stopped working for him, but Mitch didn't know that.

Now, as they were not simply passing each other but

had momentarily paused, there seemed nothing to do but introduce him to Mitch. "Professor Lehman, this is my friend, Mitchell Beers." She got it out quickly. Just as quickly, her face heated up. "Mitch . . . this is Professor Lehman."

They shook hands. "Great day, isn't it, sir?" Mitch said, staring frankly at the other man.

"Splendid. Looks like the whole college has turned out."

"It certainly does, sir."

The thump of Earthworks' drums boomed into the air.

"Well," Nicholas said with an urbane nod, "nice meeting you." An awkward moment as they maneuvered to get out of each other's way. Then, "So that's the great professor," Mitch said, as they crossed the street and entered the park.

"Why did you keep calling him sir?" They walked across the spongy grass. "It sounded so funny." Her face was still warm.

"Oh, I don't know. Respect for his great age, I suppose."

Last night she had dreamed that she told Mitch everything and he forgave her. *I forgive you,* he said. And he kissed her gently. *This is just like a movie,* she said. But then she had awakened from the dream sad instead of happy. She didn't understand that.

The park was crowded with families, students, and kids on bikes and skateboards. A man with a baby riding his shoulders passed them. "Mitch, did you see?" Nina turned to smile at the child who clutched his father's hair.

Past the swings and sandbox, they climbed on an empty seesaw. They swayed in midair for a moment, then Mitch leaned back and the board went down on his side, bobbing Nina into the air. "I haven't see-sawed for years," he said. His knees were in the air. He hunched forward, pushed his feet off the ground. Up he went. Down she came.

"Oh, lookit 'em, lookit 'em," two little girls yelled. Mitch stuck out his tongue.

Nina laughed. Odd how you felt things in layers. Laughter, eating an ice cream, bobbing like a kid on a seesaw—all on one layer. On another layer, chewing over that sudden meeting with Nicholas Lehman. God. Her heart had nearly stopped with fright. And her face—it must have gone scarlet. And then still another layer of feeling, like the soggy bottom of a poorly cooked cake: remorse, disappointment in herself. She still hadn't forgiven herself.

On the seesaw, she pushed off into the air.

Did her dream mean she should tell Mitch so she could be forgiven? Would telling make what had happened on the Oriental rug disappear? The truth an eraser, and her *Oh . . . oh . . . oh . . .* no more than chalk?

She thought back to the beginning. Someone to love —that was all she had wanted. A longing for that time when everything had been fresh and new and simple seized her.

"Mitch—" She leaned forward. "Mitch, I did it. I did it with Professor Lehman." The words flew out of her mouth. Her legs flew into the air. Horrified, she gripped the T-bar. She had said it. She had told.

What had possessed her? Mitch looked at her, not understanding. Then . . . understanding. He stood, and Nina crashed to the ground.

He was off the seesaw and away. She caught up with him at a Mr. Nice Cream truck parked at the curb. He bought an Eskimo Pie and ate it in three bites. "You did it?" he said.

"Yes . . ." Oh, Nina, dumb, naive Nina! How could you think this was going to make everything simple and sweet again?

"Why'd you tell me? Why'd you have to tell me?"

She nodded miserably. A fair question. "I wanted— I wanted to make it okay again. No secrets. And for you to understand. Mitch, I did it when Emmett—"

"I'm not listening, Nina." He hurried ahead of her. "I don't want to hear it now." He turned and walked backward. "I'm just—I'm just—" He shook his head. "I don't know, I'm just *stunned*."

"I know," she said humbly.

They passed the corner where she'd found Emmett's body. Was that why she'd done it? That was the reason, wasn't it? But then, for a moment, she was confused. Did she mean, was that why she had loved with Nicholas Lehman? Or did she mean, was that why she had now told Mitch? And which one was worse?

As they crossed the street a panhandler wearing a torn red T-shirt stepped into her path. "Hey, man, got a buck?" Nina found a quarter in her pocket. "Thank you, sister, you're a real human being."

"You don't like it," Mitch shouted, "shove it!"

They went into the building, up the stairs. A letter from Nina's mother was on the floor under the door.

"Lynell must have brought it over," Nina said. "Or maybe Sonia did. Do you think it was Sonia?" It seemed important to know.

Mitch came out of the kitchen with a can of beer. He tipped back his head, gulped beer. "You want?" He held out the can. She drank in quick little sips.

"Maybe I should go home," she said.

"What do you mean, go home?"

"Go home. Home. For the weekend or—I don't know. I could get a bus about four o'clock this afternoon."

"That's crazy. You'll go home today and come back when, tomorrow?"

She sat down, finished the beer. "I'd stay a few days. Visit with my family. No classes next week, remember? I could stay home, study for the finals."

"That's a rotten idea."

"No, I don't think so." She started pulling clothes out of the closet.

"What're you doing?" Mitch said. "Stop. Nina, it looks like you're taking everything you own. . . . Did you do it a lot?"

"What? No! Once."

"Once? Just once? Come on!"

"Once," she said. "Just once. Maybe I shouldn't come back."

"Where? To school? What do you mean?"

"No. Here. Not come back here."

"What do you mean, *here*?"

"Why do you keep saying 'What do you mean?' I mean not come back—here."

"Not come back to me? Why, Nina? Why?"

"Because I—you know why! Because of . . . because of what I did." She was almost in tears. She went into the bathroom and grabbed tampons, toothpaste, and the jar of zit cream they shared. "Is it okay if I take the zit cream?"

"Nina, am I kicking you out? No! Do you know what you're doing, Nina? You're punishing me for what you did. I should be the one walking out, but I wouldn't do that. I wouldn't hurt you that way. I wouldn't walk out on you, and you know why? Because you're not the only one."

Sitting on her suitcase, trying to zip it, Nina said, "I'm not the only one what?" Mitch bit his cheeks, as if trying not to laugh, or maybe not to cry.

"You and Lynell," she said.

He nodded.

"When? Now?"

"No, not now."

"When? *When?*"

"You know—before. When I was out of work."

"Out of work? All those weeks? *All that time?*"

"What do you mean, all that time? What kind of question—"

"I did it once," she said. "Just once. Just once, Mitch."

"I'll give you a medal! I didn't count. What do you think of that? I did it as much as I could, anytime Lynell was willing. Because I was miserable and I needed something and she—"

The ice cream and the beer were coming up on Nina. She ran into the bathroom and threw up.

Chapter Twenty-nine

Nina didn't go home. Nor did she, as she briefly thought she might, move out. Move out where? More to the point, move out why? "We both made mistakes," Mitch said. "Okay, it's not the end of the world. Let's not go overboard. I don't want you to leave, Nina. Look, now we both know. Maybe it's for the best. We can put it behind us."

A sensible point of view. They had each made some wrong moves. As in a game of checkers? But in games there was a winner, a loser. Here, as Mitch pointed out, it was a draw. *He* had done wrong; *she* had done wrong. Tit for tat. X = Y. Two wrongs didn't make a right, but surely they cancelled each other out? "We're wiping the slate clean," Mitch said. And it was in this spirit that they agreed to give themselves time. How much time they didn't spell out.

One day, alone in the apartment, Nina called home and spoke to Nancy. "I need to talk to someone."

"I'm listening," Nancy said.

"Okay," Nina said, and stopped. She didn't know where to start, what she wanted from Nancy, or even how much she wanted to tell.

"Hell-oo?" Nancy said.

Nina put her legs up on the table and, on a long indrawn breath, said, "Nance? Remember I told you about living with Mitch?"

"Sure."

"Well, it seems . . . it seems . . ." Nina sighed, banged her feet to the floor and said, "Nance, I got mixed up with someone else. It just happened once, but I told Mitch, and then—"

"You told him?" Nancy broke in. "Why'd you do that?"

"I had to. I couldn't stand the way I felt. And then he told me he—he did it, too."

"Both of you? Both of you got tight with other people?" Nina nodded as if Nancy could see her. "Did you both know you were both doing it?"

"No!"

"Well, you never know with folks is my motto. Who was it? Friends?"

"With him, yes. Me—one of my professors. I thought you could help me figure things out. I haven't had anyone really to talk to."

"Nina. I really appreciate that you—I mean, you know I can't stand being soppy, but that you came to me, it means something to me, Nina."

"I guess what I want is some—advice?" Nina said.

"I don't know. Maybe nothing, maybe just listening."

"You said you and Professor—just once?"

"Yes."

"So where's the big deal? You sound so shook. I thought you had cancer or something."

At this reminder of her grandmother, Nina said remorsefully, "Nan? Damn. I'm such an idiot. I didn't even ask about Grandma."

"Oh, she's going along as usual. Supposed to be dying, but she sure don't look like a dying lady to me. Or act like one, either. Betcha ten to one those doctors have screwed up, and she's going to live for another ten years."

"Well, give her my love."

"Sure. I'll even kiss her for you."

"Do that. I mean it."

"Okay. I mean it, too. . . . Now, listen, on the subject of you screwing around—"

"Nancy—"

"My language offends you?"

"I'm not screwing around. I think we had this conversation once before, also. And I don't like it any better this time."

"Sorry again. Okay, on the subject of your, er, problem, my advice is, you're taking it too seriously."

"It is serious. Living together—you don't think that's serious? I do. It's almost like being married, and when you're married, you don't—"

"Oh, come on," Nancy yelped. "No way is it like being married. Is that what you really think? Come on! It's not like being married the way Mom and Dad are married."

"I guess you're right," Nina said after a moment. There was a half-empty can of soda on the table. She sipped from it. "But, still, you shouldn't fool around. And we both did. That's what's so depressing." She dropped the can, wanting to spit out the flat, tasteless liquid.

"Listen, Nina, because you screwed—excuse me, made love—with two guys does not mean the world is going to topple. That was not Chicken Little's message. Did you ever ask yourself what screwing really means? It's great, sure; I wouldn't want to live without it. But it's not that holy special, either. What I mean, Nina—everybody does it, right? Everybody. And they all do it with everybody else. And so what?"

"I shouldn't have done it." It was the only thing Nina could think of to say. "I shouldn't have done it."

"So why did you? Curious?"

"No."

"Ahh, Nina, everyone is curious. If all I'd ever had was one guy, I sure would be. Hey, was it nice?"

"That's not the point."

"Are you kidding? Geez! I think you're serious. Nina, let me tell you something I've been thinking about. I've been thinking deep thoughts, sis. About life. And I've decided that my idea of life is that it's most like a humongous house."

"Life is a house?" Nina couldn't help laughing. "Nobody but you, Nancy."

"Wait, you haven't heard the rest. And in this humongous house there are parties going on. Parties in every room. Get it?"

"No."

"Well, look," Nancy said patiently. "In every room —and there are hundreds of them—there are these terrific parties, and every party is different from every other party. Now do you see? Me—I want to go to all those parties. Don't you, Nina?"

Nina had no answer.

A few nights later, waking out of a sound sleep, she saw Emmett's humped dark shape at the foot of the bed. An explosion of joy roared through her. "Emmett!" She sat up, wriggling her toes at him. He disappeared.

She sat there, staring at the darkness that was now negative darkness, negative Emmett, and thought that if Emmett hadn't gotten out of the apartment that first springlike afternoon, she would have had no reason to cry in Nicholas Lehman's office. But that, of course, would not have changed the facts of Mitch's case—of Mitch and Lynell. Of which she would have continued to be totally ignorant. And in that case, where would she be now? Made a fool of.

Sitting up in the darkness with Mitch mumbling in his sleep next to her, sleep fled Nina. The back of her neck came as alive as a hand, and she understood that Mitch, of his own will, would never have told her about himself and Lynell. It was, as he kept saying, over and done with.

Only to show her that that half hour on Nicholas Lehman's Oriental rug was no worse than his "error," had he confessed, too. Sure, they had both made mistakes. Would you be human if you didn't? Let go.

Forgive and forget. He was willing, he said, even though it hadn't been easy for him to take the news about her and Nicholas Lehman. It had rocked him hard.

Had it been any easier for her to hear about him and Lynell? In a sense, hadn't it been even harder on her? Mitch barely knew Nicholas Lehman, but Lynell was a friend. And what's more, by Mitch's own admission, the thing with Lynell had gone on for some time. *As much as I could.* Hard to forget those words! They buried themselves in her, seemed to be out of sight and forgotten, then, like worms coming up to light after a rain, they reappeared, shining and slimy, at even the mention of Lynell's name.

"Are you still mad?" Mitch asked one morning. The first Sunday in May.

"Do I act mad?"

"No, but . . . you know." He passed her the doughnuts. "You act fine," he said emphatically, "but I meant . . . underneath. Subconsciously. Are you holding a grudge against me?"

Nina dunked her doughnut in coffee and nipped at the sweet sogginess. *Forgive and forget.* She agreed to the principle, but while forgiving seemed something within her control, forgetting had so far escaped her. She wanted to forget, but she didn't. She remembered what she had done. She remembered what he had done. Faces, places, and scenes, real and imagined, made themselves too much at home in her mind.

"I don't think I'm mad anymore," she said finally.

"I'm not, either," Mitch said. "I've forgotten what happened."

"You really don't remember?"

"Well, sure I do. . . . But I don't think about it. I don't brood over it."

"I don't brood over it, either."

"That's good, I was afraid you were."

"No," she said quickly, shaking her head.

"But, still . . ." He sighed deeply. There was a little ring of sugar around his mouth that touched Nina. Made him look like a little boy. "I feel we really haven't gotten into a good place again. I wish we'd just met."

"Why? Then everything would still have to happen."

"It could be different."

"I was thinking about that. I don't know. I think it would be all the same, because you'd be you and I'd be me, and—" She shrugged. "I wouldn't want to start again. Not knowing what was coming."

"You wouldn't know. It would just be the beginning."

"So what would be the use?"

He stared at her. "You defeat me when you put on that crisp, practical voice."

"Sorry!"

"Are we going to fight?" he said in a moment.

"I hope not. I don't have the time today." She laughed a little.

"Studying again? I thought maybe we'd go out. It's a fantastic day."

"Maybe later."

"If we'd just met, you wouldn't have said *later* in that tone of voice."

"What tone of voice?"

"Forget I said it. Don't get hostile."

"I'm not getting—"

"Nina, Nina, let's play a game. Let's play we just met. I see you and I say, 'Hello! I'm Mitch Beers.' And you say—"

Nina smiled. "Hello. I'm Nina Bloom."

"Bloom?"

"Bloom."

"Nina Bloom Bloom, you're someone I'd like to kiss."

"Just what I was thinking about you."

"Well, let's do it."

They kissed, just their lips meeting. A grade-school kiss that made them both laugh.

"Again?" Mitch said.

"Again." She leaned across the table, put her hands on his shoulders, felt the strong bones beneath her fingers, and kissed him harder.

"How was that?" he asked.

"Good."

"Aww, Bloom, you can do better than that! How about on a scale of one to ten?"

"Oh . . . an eight for sure."

"Only an eight? Not a ten? Did the prof—" He cut himself off, but it was clear he'd been about to say, *Did the professor rate only an eight?*

And what would she have said? *Lynell—what did she rate?*

But neither said anything. Nina studied. Mitch went out to play basketball. Later they took a long walk. Still later they made cinnamon toast and sat up in bed, legs twined together, eating and talking and making plans.

They decided they should do more things together. From now on they'd get up early every morning and jog together. Also they'd make a real effort to keep the apartment cleaner. They agreed that Nina should look for a summer job. And maybe they would hunt for a better apartment—more space to move around in, something closer to a real home. "But near campus," Nina said. Then they discussed renting a car some weekend in June and visiting both sets of parents. "I know my mother will like you," Mitch said.

"You and my father will get along." Nina clasped her knees. This morning she had thought they were going to blow all their carefully nurtured goodwill. But they had gotten past the dangerous moment, and had a good day. And now, making plans with Mitch, she remembered exactly how she had felt when she was ten years old, on the first day of school. Shoes polished to a fare-thee-well, untouched notebook under her arm, she would set off with her head filled with promises to herself. All the disappointments still to come.

No, but what a way to think! Here it was late at night, and they were sitting up together after having made love, brushing cozily at the crumbs from their toast. So why did these traitorous little thoughts sneak in? Was she sitting here enthusiastically agreeing to everything, but not believing any of it? Too tired to pursue this line of thought any further, she pushed it out of her mind.

In some ways nothing had changed between her and

Mitch. She was still drawn to him, he could still make her laugh, and she still thought more about him than anyone else. And yet, in another way, it was all changed. There was something new, a new awareness, almost like a third person or, more accurately, another Nina, who now stood, if not between them, then alongside them at every moment. They were no longer a twosome.

A shadow had been cast. It was present, it was there, flickering, dim, but with a life of its own. Nina had been made unsure by what had happened—unsure about herself, about Mitch, about them. And there had been little changes. They no longer seemed to crowd into the bathroom together. Sometimes Nina, having studied late, slept on the couch. And mornings, rushing, grabbing a roll, books, papers, she said, "Sorry, hon, no time for breakfast."

And more and more she would remember her joy, her happiness, her deep satisfaction when she'd moved in with Mitch at having her own territory and, at last, that precious closeness and intimacy with another loved person. How much she had wanted that sense of *us*. Us. We two. A unit, self-contained. A small perfect circle. There they had been, at the center, in the heart of the heart of their own world. And nothing else had seemed to matter.

Chapter Thirty

The apartment was stuffy. Nina studied by the open window. Outside a dog barked, car horns bleated. Thinking of her first exam, which was on Tuesday afternoon, her stomach jumped. She went into the kitchen. Always ate too much when she was nervous. She gobbled a piece of bread, ate some cold frozen peas, and then searched restlessly in the cupboard. Tucked in with the cans of baked beans and chicken noodle soup, she found a can of cat food. She stared at it weakly. How could she not have seen it before this? Ages ago Mitch had gotten rid of the catbox, the extra bag of kitty litter, and the big bag of kibble. But somehow he had overlooked this one can of cat food. She shut the cupboard door on it quickly.

Moving around the apartment, unable now to sit

still, she thought about how she and Mitch kept saying to each other that everything was fine. Fine, fine, just fine! Then she thought how last night they had gone to sleep wrapped together, but this morning awakened on opposite sides of the bed, facing away from each other.

"Don't stop now." Mitch ran backward, urging Nina on. It was six o'clock Saturday morning. The streets were cool and, except for other joggers, nearly deserted. "You're doing great," he said.

"Liar," she panted.

"A couple more days and you'll be in shape."

"For what, a coffin?"

"Come on, lift those legs." He pranced around her in circles, legs high, showing off. "Come on, come on." He flicked his fingers at her.

"Quit it!"

Laughing, he ran ahead of her.

She stopped dead. "I don't like jogging," she yelled after him. "It's boring! I don't believe you when you tell me it'll give me extra energy!" Then in a sudden temper she yelled, "Did you hear me? Mitch! Did you hear me?" But he was out of sight by then, out of hearing.

That afternoon in the cheese store she ran into Lynell. "Hello, Nina." The last time Nina had seen her was the day Emmett died. "Hello, Lynell." She took her chunk of Gouda cheese to the counter.

"Ready for exams?" Lynell looked fresh in a pink smocked dress.

"Hope so. How about you?"

"I never worry about exams." She put down a box of crackers. "I had good news today. I've been accepted for a summer internship with the Philly Symphony."

"Congratulations."

"Thanks. I won't be playing. I'll be everybody's gofer. Still, it's good. The first good thing in a while. This hasn't been the best year for me. The thing with Adam, and then . . ." She looked away.

"I know what you mean," Nina said, hoping she sounded cooler than she felt. Her internal temperature was well beyond comfortable.

Outside, they smiled at each other and said good luck for exams and over the summer, and that they'd probably see each other in the fall. And all the time Nina wondered if she should say anything to Lynell about her and Mitch. Let her know *she* knew. But why? Only for revenge. Nina shrugged uncomfortably. No, she'd let it go.

"Nina—" Lynell touched her shoulder. "If I ever did anything to . . . hurt you, I'm sorry." Before Nina could recover from her surprise, Lynell walked away.

At supper that night Mitch was animated. He had heard a detailed report about a kidnapping that had some strange features. An old woman had been taken but apparently she had no money to speak of. "Who would want to kidnap her? Nobody can figure it out."

"I know . . . it's weird. . . ." Nina wasn't really listening. "I'm worried about my exams, Mitch."

"You've been studying like a demon. Relax."

"Easy for you to say. You don't have to go through it."

"That's because I gave up all that crap."

"It's not crap to me. It's important to me. Certain things are important to me. Emmett was important to me."

"Emmett? How'd he get into this?"

"I was thinking about him today. I miss him, I really miss him. I guess that's something else you can't understand, either."

"Nina, cool it."

"I hate the way you say that."

"How do I say it? I don't say it any special way."

"As if I'm hysterical! I'm cool. *Cool*."

"Okay, you're cool. A cool fool."

"What did you say?"

"Nothing. Just a joke."

"I heard you. Why'd you call me a fool?"

"I didn't, Nina; it was just something to say. Rhyming. Cool . . . fool . . ."

"You just said it again."

"Nina. Unfair! I was only trying to show you. Look, it was one of those dumb remarks. I didn't mean it about you, okay? Okay?"

"Okay," she said. "Okay. If you say so."

"Aren't you out of the shower yet?" Mitch called.

"Another minute."

"It's already been ten minutes."

"Mitch, I just stepped in." And then, controlling her irritation, "I saw Lynell yesterday."

He put his head inside the shower curtain. "So?"

"So nothing." She pulled the curtain closed.

"Why do you keep bringing up Lynell? I don't

want to hear about her. I don't think it helps anything."

She shampooed her hair. "I was just giving you a bit of news."

"Would you like me to bring up your professor every two minutes?"

"It's the first time I've mentioned Lynell's name! And he's not *my* professor." She threw down the plastic shampoo bottle. "The way you say that!"

"He's sure not my professor. I saw him the other day. He crossed the street. Good thing."

"What are you saying? That you'd fight him or something?"

"Yeah, or *something*."

"Are you going to get steamed up every time you see him? You're bound to run into him."

"Well, I can't see him and feel blank!"

"You talk as if everything were one-sided. How do you think I felt seeing Lynell?"

"That's different, Nina. A man's feelings aren't like a woman's."

"Oh, Mitch!"

"No, I mean it. What I did with Lynell is one thing. And what you did with *him* is something else."

"You mean, worse."

"You said it."

"I don't believe this. That's crazy! And you know something else crazy? All this time and you never even asked me why it happened. There was a reason."

"I don't want to know, Nina. I really . . . don't . . . want . . . to . . . know."

"But I want to tell you! You told me your reason.

You said you were depressed being out of work. Well, I was depressed, too. I was depressed because—"

"Nina, you could have the best reason in the world, and it would still cut me to pieces knowing what you did."

"That's not fair," she said.

His eyes darkened. "It's the way I feel."

"Well, then, I hate your feelings!"

"We're fighting again," he said.

"We're not fighting," she said. "We're not fighting! Every time someone raises their voice, you call it fighting." She wrapped herself in a towel. "It's all yours." Stepping out of the tub, she took another towel for her hair.

"Listen . . . I want to ask you something," he said. "How'd you feel the first time you saw him—afterward?"

"Embarrassed," she said tightly. "Scared! Stupid! Attracted! Afraid! Okay, okay? Is your curiosity satisfied?"

"Why are you getting so mad?"

"I told you, it was just once, but you harp on it."

"I don't mean to," he said. "I really don't mean to but—" He dropped his jeans on the floor and stepped into the shower.

"But what?" Nina said.

"Nothing. Forget it."

"Come on, Mitch!"

"Nina, it's stupid. You don't want to hear it. I'm sorry I started this, if I'm the one who started it."

Nina toweled her hair hard. These fights of theirs! Over before they began. She couldn't grab on to anything, couldn't find a hard, solid reason for that little ball of anger sitting in her stomach. Mitch, with his reasonableness—reasonable-sounding even when he was unreasonable—seemed to slip through her fingers. Just at the moment when he got her raging mad, when she finally had something to pin on him, he would do a little dance, sidestep, apologize, fade away. *I didn't mean . . . sorry . . . forget it. . . .* And she was left as unsatisfied as a hungry person who'd had a plate of food snatched away just as she began to eat.

"Mitch, I want to know what you were going to say."

"Nina—"

"Say—it!"

Silence from behind the shower curtain. Then, so low she had to strain to hear, he said, "I keep thinking about you, you and him. Thinking about the two of you. Not every minute, but enough . . ."

"Well, stop," she said. "Just stop thinking about it. Because there's nothing to think about anymore."

"I can't help it," he said humbly.

"There you go again! You start something, and then you stop. And another thing, you're so sensitive, you've got me afraid to even say his name."

"Say it. I don't give a damn about that."

"Neither do I, then." She pulled open the curtain. "Nicholas," she breathed into his face. "Nicholas, Nicholas."

Water streamed over Mitch's shoulders. "Don't, Nina. Please don't. Please!"

Nina laughed miserably. "All right, Mitch, I won't. I won't say his name again."

Chapter Thirty-one

On Thursday Nina took her last two exams, then spent the rest of the day leaving job applications in stores. A hard, cold rain fell. It was late when she got home, and she was wet and weary. Their apartment was cozy, lit up. Mitch was in the big chair, reading and eating a slice of pizza. "Hi," he said. "I bought supper. Why so late?"

"Looking for work. I went to at least a dozen places."

"Have some pizza. Are you starved?" She shook her head. The greasy cardboard box reminded her of that day she'd come back, crampy and tired, and found Lynell here. How distant all that seemed now. How ignorant and naive she appeared to herself in retrospect.

"Any luck with work?"

"Nothing." She hung her slicker over a chair. "I should have done this months ago. All the summer jobs are already sewed up. I blew it." She didn't remind him that she hadn't gone job hunting because she'd counted on summer work from Nicholas Lehman.

"How was the exam?" Mitch asked.

"Exams, plural," Nina said, going into the kitchen. "I think I did okay."

"*Return of the Pink Panther* is playing at the Sneller. Want to go? No studying tonight, Nina. No more studying until next semester. You ought to celebrate."

She took a can of cat food from the cupboard, got the can opener. "I can't believe it's over. Tell me it's over. Tell me it's really true."

"It's true, it's true," Mitch said, standing in the doorway.

"Now I'll worry until I get my marks."

"That's what I call useless. Nina, what are you doing?"

"Getting Emmett's food," she said. Stricken, she looked at Mitch. "I was going to feed him, Mitch. I was going to feed Emmett. I forgot . . . blanked it right out. . . . I thought he was here, I was going to call him. Come on, Emmett, time for supper! Mitch, did you see what I was *doing*?"

He took the can and threw it into the garbage. "I thought we got rid of all that. I thought I threw everything out."

"You didn't. You didn't throw out everything."

"Nina, what are you crying for? Don't, Nina. God, I'm sorry. Nina, Emmett's gone. You've been used to it for weeks."

"No, it's not about Emmett," she said. "It's not him. I'm not crying about him. It's us."

She blew her nose in a napkin. "It's not working, Mitch. Staying together—it's not working."

"What are you talking about?" His face reddened. He threw the can opener back into the drawer with a clatter.

"That's what I mean," Nina said.

"What? Make sense!" He slammed the door shut with his hip.

"And *that*. You're mad. So am I. I try not to be, but I am. And we don't trust each other anymore."

"That's not true," he said quickly. He pushed his hands through his hair, making it stand up in wild curls. "I trust you. Why shouldn't I? All that other stuff is in the past."

"Maybe I'm not saying it right. It's a state of mind I'm talking about. Sort of a cloud in your mind—"

"You don't know what's in my mind."

"Okay, my mind. A cloud in *my* mind. As if I don't . . ." She spoke slowly. ". . . don't really know you anymore. Maybe never did. What you're thinking about me . . . or yourself."

"I'm thinking the same things I always thought."

"I guess I'm not saying it right," she said again. "But I know what I mean." She'd opened the can, opened everything up. Then he'd thrown away the

can, but couldn't throw away what she was saying
about them: that *it*—all that stuff, as Mitch put it—
wasn't "in the past."

"Mitch, it's right here with us," she said. "It's been
with us every minute. What you did. What I did. I
didn't forget. I wanted to. I tried to! But even when I
wasn't thinking about it, it was there in the back of
my mind. Sort of snagged. Today I saw a plastic bag
caught in a tree, and I thought, Oh, you see that every
spring, bags and newspapers and junk caught in tree
branches. And then I wondered if it was the same
plastic bag from last winter. Do you know what I'm
saying?"

"Great metaphor," he said. "Your mind's a tree and
there's a plastic bag stuck in it. You know what you can
do with that bag! Stick it over your head!" He hit his
fist on the wall. "We made some mistakes. We both
made some little mistakes, and you—"

"Stop it! Don't say that again. Little mistake! Not
good enough." In her agitation she was sweating and
shivering. "Living together . . . okay, it's not love,
honor, and cherish forever, but it's something, isn't it?
I thought it was *something*. So did you. You know you
did."

"I still do," he said.

"Then why call it a little mistake? Don't you feel
crummy about it?"

"Sure I do. But what good does it do to beat ourselves?"

She shook her head, her lips pressed together. She
couldn't stop shivering. "I just go on feeling so *bad*.

Thought I knew you, thought the person you are would never have done that with Lynell—"

He sagged against the door. "Nobody knows anybody, not really, Nina. This is a lonely world. Haven't you figured that one out yet?"

"Lonely even when you live with someone? I don't want to believe that, Mitch. It hurts too much!"

"I thought you were a realist, my friend." He almost smiled. "My practical, working-class chick, you can't make things not be the way they are by refusing to believe them."

"Maybe we just don't see things in the same light, Mitch."

After a moment he said, "You're more of a dreamer than I realized."

"You call it dreaming because I feel rotten about what we did?"

"Too damn bad I told you about the thing with Lynell," he said, almost to himself. "Did you have to know? Did I do you any favors?"

"We keep saying the *thing* with Lynell. The *thing* with Nicholas. I hate that. It's such a lie."

"What do you want to call it? The *fornication*? The *adultery*?"

She flushed. "Did you always get your kicks mocking me?"

"Ahh, Nina—!" He walked away, came back. "I'm just trying to stir you up, wake you up. You see a can of cat food and, all of a sudden, the world is falling apart. Our world. Why now? Why this minute?"

She looked out of the rain-streaked window, remembering other rainy days, remembering Sunday breakfasts . . . music on the street . . . drinking wine from a green gallon jug . . . a pillow fight . . . eating cinnamon toast in bed. . . .

What if she and Mitch had known more? Or believed in each other more? Believed enough to stay away from other people, from Lynell and Nicholas? Would that have saved them? Or was it not that simple? Was it that they hadn't loved each other enough? That what they had thought and said was love was— something else. A little love. Only the beginning of love, not the real thing, not the lasting thing.

She turned away from the window. "What I'm thinking— It's time. I have to move out."

"Move out?" he said, as if he'd never heard the words.

"We said we'd give ourselves time. We did, but . . ." She shook her head.

"Where will you go?" he said, his face drawing down.

"Home . . ." Back home with her parents, who would never know that "little" Nina had lived with her lover. She wondered if life had been easier for her mother, growing up with such straight, clear yes-you-mays and no-you-may-nots that she would as soon have robbed a bank as lived with Nina's father without marriage.

And all these years that her parents had stayed together—was it happily? Or was it *despite*? Despite their longings for other people? Despite their separateness? Their differences?

She tried to see them as they must once have been.

Could see them only as they were—Mom and Dad. Coupled. Linked. Joined forever. Maybe after all these years, all that was between them—time, events, children, grief and joy—had grown back in a circular motion into some of the love Nina longed to believe they had once had for each other.

"It was good," Mitch said. "Nina, it can be good again."

Her head began to ache. Easier for her when he was angry, when she could meet his anger with hers. "Mitch, it's all gone. . . ."

"Neenah . . ." The old soft way of saying her name. "Nina, all because you opened a can of cat food?" He planted himself in front of her. His face worked. "I know I did wrong. I admitted it—"

"Not you. *We*. We both did it. When it was good, we did that together. And now, when it's not good, we did that, too."

"What do you want from me now? What do you want me to do?"

She held out her hands hopelessly. "Nothing," she said, sadly. "I don't want you to do anything. Not anymore."

"A lousy can of cat food." He opened the cupboard, swept it clear of cans. Cans hit the counter, rolled onto the floor. "Lousy can of cat food." He kicked a can across the room, opened the door, kicked it down the steps.

"Mitch . . ." Nina stood in the doorway, laughing helplessly. "Mitch, you madman!"

"Do you mean it?" he yelled. "You're moving out?"

She heard a door opening on the floor above.

"Yes!" she yelled back.

"You won't change your mind?"

"I can't!"

He came bounding back up the steps, ran toward her, his face wet, gleaming as if lighted from within by joy. But he was crying. She had never seen him cry. She held out her arms, held him, and cried with him.

Chapter Thirty-two

"Mitch?" From the couch, Nina leaned over and touched Mitch's shoulder. "It's morning. Are you awake."

"Sort of."

"Did I wake you up?"

"Don't you always?"

"See how much better off you're going to be without me?"

They had talked late into the night. Nina's timing, as Mitch said only half sarcastically, was perfect. "Your exams are over, you haven't got a job, so what's holding you here? No reason for you not to go home. You could go tomorrow."

"You sound anxious to get rid of me."

"It's true in a way. Now that you're going, I want to see you gone."

"Okay! I'll go tomorrow. Fine!"

"I'll help you pack."

That had been the low moment of the night, the closest they had come to lashing out at each other. But they had stopped themselves, agreeing they would try not to part in bitterness. "Harder for me than you," Mitch had pointed out. "You're leaving me. I'm the left-ee."

Nothing to say to that. Nothing to say to a lot of things.

For hours last night they'd gone over and over the same territory. When they started remembering the good times, they had cried again. By then they were both exhausted and finally went to sleep, holding hands between couch and bed, like a couple of kids lost in the woods.

Mitch didn't go in to work that morning; instead he hung around as Nina sorted and packed. She'd take home only what she needed and could carry. Mitch had promised to bring her household goods, such as they were, to Sonia to store until the fall, when Nina would figure out where she was going to live.

"What are you going to do, Mitch?" she said, taking an armload of shirts out of the closet. "Are you going to stay on here, in this apartment?"

"Why not?"

"Well, I thought you didn't like living around the college."

He straddled a chair. "Maybe I will move. After a while I guess I'll find someone else. Maybe she won't like living here, either. Does that bother you, Nina? That I'll get another girl friend? Does that bother you even a little bit?"

Nina wanted to deny it, but it did bother her. Mitch serious about another girl? Yeah, it bothered her. She dumped socks and underwear into a suitcase. "It doesn't matter if it bothers me or not."

"I want it to bother you."

"Okay, it does!"

"Good!"

"Yeah, points for you." Her eyes were sore. Not enough sleep.

"You want some lunch?" Mitch said. "I'll make you a toasted cheese with onions."

"Add some tomatoes."

"My last service," he said, going into the kitchen.

"It sounds like a funeral."

He came to the door. "In a way, it is a funeral, isn't it?"

Nina stopped in the middle of folding a scarf. "I guess you're right," she said at last.

She was almost ready to leave. Suitcases packed, knapsack open for last-minute things. The radio was tuned to a news station. "A religious cult known as All God's Children has forecast the end of the world for three forty-five P.M. today."

"Precisely," Mitch said, switching off the radio.

"Good thing you didn't go in to work. You wouldn't want to miss that."

They smiled wanly at each other.

❖   ❖   ❖

Nina washed her face, combed her hair. "You don't have to come to the bus station with me, Mitch."

"You'll need help with all that junk." He glanced at her. "What are you doing now?"

"Cutting my toenails."

"Now?"

"I noticed they were growing too long, and I've started wearing sandals again," she explained.

He looked at his watch. "Do you realize you have a bus to catch in a little over an hour."

"Plenty of time," she said, snipping carefully.

"You're weird, Bloom. You really are weird."

"That's why you love me so," she teased. Then, hearing her words, she blushed deeply, as if she'd said something unforgivably rude.

"It's really hard to believe I won't be coming back here," Nina said, locking the door.

"You can still change your mind."

She held out the key to him. He grabbed her suitcase, ran ahead of her down the stairs.

She caught up with him. "Mitch—we stayed together six months. That's not so bad, is it?"

"Seven months. Your arithmetic is lousy. November, December, January—"

"It's May, isn't it? You're right."

"I thought it would be more than seven months," he said. "I wanted it to be more than seven months."

"So did I."

"Seven years would have been nice."

"How about seventeen? Can you imagine it?" She

went out the door. "I don't know how people do it."

"Why not seventy?" Mitch said in her ear.

"Seventy." Nina shifted her knapsack. "Who's a dreamer now?" She started off, walking fast, head thrust forward. Above her, the sky was wide, and blue as a plate.